Trust No Man 2

Lock Down Publications
& Ca$h Presents
Trust No Man 2
A Novel by *Ca$h*

Lock Down Publications

P.O. Box 1482
Pine Lake, Ga 30072-1482

Visit our website at **www.lockdownpublications.com**

Cover design and layout by: Marion Designs
Book interior design by: Shawn Walker
Edited by: Shawn Walker

Stay Connected with Us!

Text **LOCKDOWN** to 22828 to stay up-to-date with new releases, sneak peaks, contests and more…

Submission Guideline.

Submit the first three chapters of your completed manuscript to ldpsubmissions@gmail.com, subject line: Your book's title. The manuscript must be in a .doc file and sent as an attachment. Document should be in Times New Roman, double spaced and in size 12 font. Also, provide your synopsis and full contact information. If sending multiple submissions, they must each be in a separate email.

Have a story but no way to send it electronically? You can still submit to LDP/Ca$h Presents. Send in the first three chapters, written or typed, of your completed manuscript to:

LDP: Submissions Dept
Po Box 1482
Pine Lake, Ga 30072

DO NOT send original manuscript. Must be a duplicate.

Provide your synopsis and a cover letter containing your full contact information.

Thanks for considering LDP and Ca$h Presents.

Ca$h

CHAPTER 1

Mafuckaz better beware!

That's all I kept saying to myself as I drove to the car wash on Georgia Avenue to have my whip washed and detailed.

If niggaz thought they could get away with bangin' me up, putting me in the hospital with a busted head, a broken jaw and cracked ribs and not have to feel my heat, then they had the game twisted!

I was out of the hospital now. Busted up, but alive and ready to turn the streets of ATL into a war zone.

I still had the loot on me that had been in my pocket the night I was taken to the hospital. The emergency workers had given it to Inez. She had returned it to me as soon as I was awake and coherent.

After my whip was spotless, shining and smelling brand new, I paid and tipped the boys. Then I drove to Decatur to my crib to check on Cheryl, my daughters and my bank.

I knew Cheryl would be mad because I hadn't told her I was banged up in the hospital, but that was the least of my concerns.

I'ma find those niggaz that banged me up, and show 'em how the fuck I get down! I thought as I pulled into my apartment complex, parked, got out of my ride and headed up to my apartment.

As soon as I opened the door and stepped inside, I knew something wasn't right. The only sound in the apartment was water dripping from the faucet in the kitchen sink. I followed the sound. When I reached the kitchen, the freezer door was ajar, leaving a puddle of water on the floor.

The chicken boxes where I kept some of my stash were scattered about the kitchen counter, empty as fuck!

My safes! My million-dollar stash!

In a panic, I dashed to the bedroom to check the closet. The closet door stood wide open. I held my breath and peeked inside.

Both safes were gone.

Oh, hell naw!

So was my cache of guns.

My clothes were cut up and strewn all over the bedroom.

That lowdown bitch! Some nigga put her up to this! My million-dollar stash was gone! I screamed like a madman through my wired mouth.

The pain from my cracked ribs hit me so hard that I crumpled to the floor.

After the pain lessened a bit, I was able to get to my feet. I stumbled back into the kitchen where I noticed a letter stuck on the refrigerator door. It was held in place with one of those small, plastic smiley faces. I snatched the letter off of the door and began reading.

Youngblood,

Don't bother trying to find us, nigga, 'cause you never will. You didn't want me in your life, so now I'm out, me and your daughters! See, we're a package deal. You can't have them and not me! I give you credit for loving Chante and Eryka, but you treated me like shit!

Nigga, you made me stop loving you after money made you stop loving me. Money changed you, nigga! That's why I'm taking all of your dough. Maybe without riches, you'll treat women nicer.

Oh, just so you know, I have a man who loves me. He's the Haitian nigga you caught knocking on the door that time. Yep, caught your ass slippin', not up on your game. I may have gotten fat, but your ass got dumb!

Again, don't try to find us, we're moving out of the country and never coming back. Dag, motherfucker I hate you! But who's crying now? It sho' ain't me.

Thanks to you, I'm a rich, fat bitch!

Later nigga,

Cheryl, Eryka and Chantè

Cheryl's letter smashed me!

I fell to my knees in the puddle of water and cried like a baby. The bitch had run off with my two little princesses and all my bank.

Bitch, you think stealing my dough is gonna make me nicer? Hell the fuck naw! It's gonna make me even more of a killa. Startin' with your fam'.

Inez could tell something was wrong as soon as I walked in her house. My eyes were red and my body dragged. All of my swagger was gone.

"What's wrong?" she asked, alarmed.

For a long time, I couldn't answer. I just sat there, staring into space. She got up and sat on the floor at my feet and laid her head on my knee. My blankness must've warned her that whatever was the matter was serious.

After a long silence, mumbling through my mouth wire, I told her what I had discovered at my apartment and showed her Cheryl's letter, leaving out the exact dollar amount that was taken.

"She shouldn't have taken your money. All she had to do was leave," Inez said, her voice was compassionate. "He probably put her up to it," she added.

I didn't respond. What was there to say? I had already considered that, but what difference did it make? Either way, my money was still gone. My two lil' princesses were stolen away from me. I couldn't blame the Haitian nigga. He couldn't have known about the money unless Cheryl told him. Cheryl was to blame, although I'd kill 'em both if I ever found them. But with my million dollars in their grip, they'd definitely be hard to find.

"I still have most of that fifty thousand dollars you gave me. Plus, I have some money put up," Inez said. "Do you want that?"

"Just hold on to it, shawdy. Shit gon' be a'ight." But I wasn't sure it would be. Still, Inez earned major props for offering me all that she had.

I was in a trance, a deep state of denial. I mumbled through my wired mouth for Inez to roll up a blunt and blow me a shotgun.

"You sure you can smoke?" Her concern for me was genuine.

Inhaling the smoke from the 'dro set my lungs on fire. My whole insides felt aflame but then the pain mellowed and the weed high mixed with the pain pills I'd taken earlier had me drifting off to sleep.

I dreamt I still had a million dollars but when I woke up a few hours later, reality smacked me back to the present.

I then gathered up some of my gear, the medical supplies I'd needed and one of the guns I kept under Inez's couch.

Before I left, I told her I wouldn't feel comfortable staying at her crib until I knew who was responsible for putting me in the hospital. She was probably safe 'cause if my enemies wanted to harm her, they would've done it already, but I needed to be sure.

She told me she'd probably go stay at her mother's or with a girlfriend until I was sure she'd be safe at home. "Where will you stay?" she asked.

"With Lonnie, probably."

"Or with Juanita?"

"Maybe, "I admitted. "But if I do, it'll just be a safe place to lay my head until I can figure out my next move. It won't be about sex. Real talk, I never slept with her. That was the last thing on my mind."

I trust you, boo. Just don't forget about us." She looked down at her belly. My seed inside hadn't grown enough to make it poke out yet.

I mumbled through the wire. "I'll have everything back in order soon. In the meantime, I'll call you every day."

"She scribbled her Ma Duke's and girlfriend's numbers on a piece of paper and pushed it in my palm.

When I left, I called Juanita. She didn't answer her cell phone, so I left a message on her voicemail. Ten minutes later, she called back. I answered the ringing payphone and told her I decided to accept part of her offer. I needed a place to stay while I recovered from my injuries.

She immediately left work and met me at her house. After helping me put my things in the guest room, she ran a tub full of hot water and suggested I get in and relax.

The bathtub had power jet sprays that did my sore ribs a world of therapy. While I soaked in the hot, soothing water, Juanita put fresh Epsom salt in her palm and sprinkled it around in the water.

"That'll help with the soreness," Juanita said. Then she put a fresh bandage on the wound in the back of my head.

A while later, she cooked boneless fried fish, potatoes, green beans and put it all in a blender until it was fine enough for me to suck through a straw.

After dinner, I told her what Cheryl had done and showed her the letter. As with Inez, I didn't reveal to Juanita the amount of money Cheryl had ran off with. The shit hurt to even think about.

Juanita read the letter. When she was done, she asked if I thought Cheryl would ever come back.

"I doubt it."

"So, you'll never see your daughters again?"

"Probably not," I mumbled, too hurt to say more.

Juanita said that it didn't matter if I didn't have a dime, she still wanted me to move away with her, start a new life and leave the streets behind. She suggested I sell all but one of my cars while she was put her Viper up for sale, allowing us to bank the money with the other she had saved.

We would only need one car, at least for a while. And if I didn't find a decent job right away, she said, she would get a part-time job to help out, something other than exotic dancing.

"We can rent a cheap one-bedroom apartment," Juanita said. "It won't be what we've gotten used to, but we both grew up in the projects. We'll adapt. And we'll have each other."

She said at least I wouldn't have to worry about being killed or sent to prison. In a few years, we'd be doing better and it would be worth all the sacrifices once she got her degree and started practicing medicine. In the meantime, I could go back to school or maybe build up my own business.

With what? I wondered.

"Haven't you ever wanted to be anything besides a hustler?" she asked.

"Not that I can remember."

"Well," Juanita said, not giving up, "I still have a few more weeks to change your mind."

CHAPTER 2

Lonnie was back in town and riding shotgun with me. I'd told him everything that had gone down while he and Delina were in NY, keeping my words to a minimum since my shit was wired.

We rapped about Blue and how he killed the Ribs Lady adopted daughter. Blue was facing the death penalty for it. Lonnie said he wished he could've gotten to Blue before the police did. He would've killed the nigga himself, to save Delina and the kids the drama.

We both shook our heads, not knowing what else to say about it.

As for Cheryl, he said the bitch needed to be put in a body bag. I hadn't told him how much was in the safes, but he still doubted she would ever return to Atlanta. He said that if the bitch wasn't in Haiti, she was probably on some island in Jamaica or the West Indies.

"If she hasn't left the United States, you can track her down with her social security number," Lonnie said. "That dumb ho won't think to establish a false identity." But I was never going to underestimate any woman again. Cheryl had to be some kind of smart to get ghost with my bank.

Lonnie believed Blondie and Little Gotti were probably responsible for my kidnapping. But how would they have known where Inez lived, unless they had us followed from The Player's Ball that night.

It then dawned on me that I'd told Blondie my name was Youngblood when she'd called me Popeye at The Player's Ball. Yet, at the sports bar, I'd told her man my name was Terrence. Both were the truth if Little Gotti had the means of checking it out. *But had that small discrepancy caused him to believe I was lying to cover my ass?*

13

But how would he have known I was in Englewood the day I was abducted? Who could've known that and had time enough to plan the abduction?

Fuck it! I'd ride on *all* my enemies, that way I was sure to get the guilty one. But first things first. I rang the doorbell.

"Who is it?" the woman asked.

"Terrence," I answered as clearly as my wired mouth allowed.

I heard the lock turn, and the door opened just a crack. Lonnie's foot kicked it loose from the security chain and knocked the woman backwards, but she didn't fall. Nor did she scream. She just stood there, petrified, like a deer caught in headlights.

I pointed the gun at Cheryl's mother.

"Tell me where Cheryl is!" My voice was low, demanding.

Lonnie closed the front door, grabbed her by the throat and pushed her toward the stairs, damn near lifting her clear off her feet. His gloved hand dug into her throat as he forced her up the stairs and into the bathroom. When he released her from his grip, Cheryl's mother coughed violently. As soon as the bitch caught her breath, I nodded to Lonnie. My partner grabbed her by the back of her hair, forced her over the commode and pushed her face down in the toilet water.

I nodded again and he yanked her head up.

The bitch was coughing, crying and gasping for breath all at the same time. "Tell me where Cheryl's at!" I said for the second time.

"I—don't—know," she cried.

I nodded to Lonnie and he dunked her head in the toilet again. This time for thirty seconds. When he brought her up, she was choking brutally, desperate for air.

"Where's Cheryl?" I asked again.

"I swear—I—don't—know!"

I punched her in the eye.

"Drown this bitch!" I said to Lonnie. And he would've if I hadn't told him to bring her back up when her body started twitching aggressively and her legs kicked at the air.

She lay on the bathroom tile gasping for air, spitting up toilet water.

Her blouse was soaked. Her hair was wild and stringy. Her left eye was swollen halfway shut already.

I put my size ten in the center of her back and pointed the gun down at her.

"Last time," I said. "Where's Cheryl?"

"Wait! Don't—kill—me," she cried. She begged me to let her show me a letter Cheryl had left under her front door. I led her to her bedroom, pulling her by the hair.

Cheryl's letter to her mother read:

Dear Mama,

This is the last time you'll ever hear from me. I've taken the children and moved far away. I'm sure you won't miss me or your grandbabies, being that you never loved us or wanted us around anyway.

I remember how mean you used to be to me when Daddy was at work. When he died, I missed him. You couldn't wait for me to grow up so you could be rid of me! I don't hate you, though. It takes too much energy to hate more than one person at a time, and right now all my energy goes into hating Youngblood.

Speaking of him, he'll probably try to hurt you because I took a lot of money from him, as well as taking Eryka and Chantè away. Be sure to let someone know that if something happens to you, Terrence did it! I threw away all his guns so he couldn't

15

come over there and shoot you for thinking you know where I've gone, but he can easily get more guns.

Anyway, I've met someone who loves me and my girls. I'll be a good mother to my children, unlike you were to me! Well, I'll bring this letter to a close. You always told me I talked too much!

Cheryl,
(Daddy's little girl)
P.S.
I'm never coming back!

I folded up the letter and put it in my pocket. I stared Cheryl's mother in her swollen eye and said, "If I get arrested, he'll come back and kill you!" I gestured toward Lonnie, who smiled menacingly. "I'm gonna find your daughter one of these days." It was a threat more than a promise. "You can bet on that!"

I left there determined not to rest until I had fulfilled that vow.

For the next few weeks, I laid low. I wasn't trying to be seen in the streets with my mug swollen and my jaw wired shut. Haters would've loved to see a young nigga banged up and vulnerable. If I wasn't out with Lonnie trying to ride on my enemies, I was either chillin' with Inez or at Juanita's crib laying low. But my mind was in constant motion and my mood was dark because that bitch, Cheryl, had ganked my entire bank.

I can't even begin to describe the feeling of being rich one minute and then right back to having nothing! It felt like I had dreamt I was rich, only to wake up and realize I was still struggling. But the shit hadn't been no goddamn dream. The shit was real! I had let a bitch rob me for my whole stash without having to draw a gat!

I realized I committed two cardinal sins: One, I took shit for granted, and two, I underestimated a woman's scorn.

I had only eight G's in my pocket, a tricked-out Lexus truck I could sell for a decent penny and a brand new Benz drop that would sell for even more than the Lexus. Plus, Inez had fifty grand. But when I added it all up, it came to, probably, less than 130 grand, 150 tops. No comparison to the mil' and change Cheryl had *ganked* me for.

The only choice I had was to go back to robbing niggaz, but I knew I'd never hit another big lick like that again. *How was I supposed to look forward to robbing for small money again?* Doing hits for Rich Kid wasn't steady enough, and wouldn't garner the type of loot I had lost. Plus, I was seeing him through different eyes these days.

My other option was to get down with what Juanita was stressing. But how could I trust a bitch after what Shan and Cheryl had done? Squaring up and going legit wasn't a young nigga's style. I couldn't walk away from the streets when I had the upper hand. *How in hell could I walk away now when I had just gotten knocked on my ass?*

Anyway, what was I supposed to do with Inez? Not only was she carrying my seed, she was carrying my secrets. The way I saw it, I had no choice but to stay in the streets.

Maybe I would have chosen the route Juanita proposed if it hadn't required such a sudden and drastic change from what I'd been doing all of my life or if it wouldn't have placed me in the unenviable position of being so dependent on her. After all, we may have grown up in the same projects, but I didn't know her that well.

Where would it leave me if one day, after she became a doctor, the bitch woke up and decided I wasn't the best thing since cell phones no more? And what type of nigga chose to be dependent on a female? Pimps maybe. But those clowns had played out along with Jheri curls.

17

The few that were trying to keep the mack game alive were witnessing crack driving the price of pussy so low it now cost less than a Happy Meal.

In retrospect, maybe I was just searching for convenient excuses not to leave the streets. *Whatever!* I do know that even while chillin' at Juanita's house and getting to know her better and watching her prepare to leave Atlanta and its unforgiving fast life, I never seriously thought of going away with her.

Juanita had placed an ad in the newspaper announcing a house for sale, so mafuckaz were occasionally calling and coming by to browse the furniture and whatnots. She was also selling all of her designer clothes, shoes, and exotic dancer costumes. She said that when she left the city, she'd take nothing with her but the clothes on her back, her bank book and the strength to pursue her dreams.

How could a nigga argue with that?

Fall was giving way to winter. It was chilly at night. Some of those nights Juanita would light the fireplace and we would sit watching the flames lick at the fake logs. We'd talk about all the people the hood had swallowed up. I'd mostly listen. My mind was there but in a million other places, too. We'd also listen to Maxwell, Eryka Badu and Juanita's favorite, Jill Scott.

When I was tired of love songs, I'd turn the fireplace off and replace melancholy music with whatever rap CDs I could find in Juanita's collection.

She'd get up and try to dance. I'd laugh so hard my ribs would hurt, and it would feel like my jaw had re-fractured. Juanita might've been one of the best strippers in the Dirty South, but she had white girl moves when it came to regular dancing.

I'd turn off the music before I laughed myself back into the hospital, and we'd drift off to our own private thoughts.

Sometimes I'd get up and go sleep in the guest room, and other times I'd fall asleep on the floor, with Juanita in my arms.

If my heart wasn't made of concrete, I might've fallen in love with Juanita.

As it was, we just enjoyed the moment, knowing the day was coming fast when all her things would be sold and she'd drive away.

I called Inez daily so she would know our bond was still strong. I'd scoop her from by her mom's crib, where she was at most of the time, or have her meet me at *her* spot. If I felt her trust in me beginning to wane a bit, I'd take her to a motel and show her that my interest in her was as strong as ever.

I couldn't kiss or eat her, and even though it hurt my ribs to fuck too hard or too long, I needed Inez to know that Juanita hadn't been draining me. I was sure she didn't believe I wasn't sexing Juanita, but to her credit, she never once fussed about it.

I reassured her every time I talked to her, or saw her, that things would be back to normal before long. She was anxious to go back to living at her own place because she wasn't happy having to stay with someone else. She asked again if I wanted the money she had put up. Again, I told her to just hold on to it.

"I'm not having nightmares anymore," she announced, sounding relieved that the demons that had entered her dreams after setting up King for me to jack and murk were no longer haunting her in her sleep.

"That's good," I said. "How's my baby?" I asked patting her stomach.

She responded, "My doctor says everything is fine, but I have to stop smoking weed."

I asked her how the doctor knew she smoked weed.

"I told her," Inez smiled. "She's cool."

Ca$h

CHAPTER 3

Lonnie told me that he had seen Murder Mike and that Murder had given him a number and told him to tell me to get in touch with him. I took the number and put it in my back pocket. I'd get with Murder later.

"Oh, I seen Shan yesterday," he said. "She told me to tell you Lil' T has been acting up at school and you need to come by there and talk to him."

"Yeah?" I mumbled, but all that would have to wait.

I wasn't trying to let my son see me bruised and banged up. To him, I was Superman, indestructible! I couldn't ruin his image of his pops.

Besides, ain't no way I was letting Shan or her powder head nigga, Shotgun Pete, see me not shining and on point. Niggaz wouldn't see me until I was well and had straightened my biz.

They'd hear about me, though, I thought to myself. *Starting tonight!*

I launched two fire bombs through the window of the sports bar, just seconds before Lonnie unleashed his. The four Molotov cocktails instantly erupted into small fires, igniting the bottles behind the bar. I wanted to watch the building explode; however, I knew better than to stick around.

Burning down Little Gotti's sports bar was just the beginning, sort of like a jab before the big punch. I'd get his white bitch next, make her take me to him and his lovely stash.

Why kill 'em without robbin' them first? The bitch should've let things stay as they were. Now the ante had been upped!

"Let's see if you and your man can play the high stakes game of murder!" I would've said to the bitch, had I been the type of nigga to give out warnings or idle threats, but I wasn't that type of nigga.

When my enemy saw me, the rest had been already written. *Didn't these fools in the streets know better than to wake a sleeping beast?*

My sister's boyfriend, Glen, was gonna feel my rage, too. Him and any other mafucka I suspected of causing me harm. They all would feel the rage inside of me, my thirst for blood.

***

As the weeks passed, the weather continued to change. Daylight Savings had demanded time be set back an hour, making the days shorter and the nights longer. Giving a night stalker, like myself, even more time to hunt and capture the prey.

So far, Little Gotti and his bleach blond, white bitch were outrunning their death warrants, but time was always on the side of the hunter. If my thirst for blood and revenge got too strong to wait, I could easily pay Glen a visit, first. He was always easy to find, basically a sitting duck.

Time had also taken the swelling out of my face and the soreness from my ribs. The gash in my head had healed, with hair beginning to grow in its place. My jaw was still wired closed; otherwise, I was almost as good as new.

Still, I hadn't been seen in the streets, causing mad rumors to circulate and take flight: *I was dead. In prison. Running scared. Blah. Blah. Blah.*

I couldn't say a few of the rumors didn't vex me. A street nigga never liked mafuckaz to think he was running scared. Unless it's by design, and he was just waiting to strike.

I heard all of the rumors from a distance. I was just biding my time.

Time. It went backwards, it went forward, but it never stood still or waited for anyone, which meant the time had come for me to make a choice.

Juanita and I watched the two men load the last of her bed-room furnishings onto the U-Haul trailer. One of the mover's wives carried the bedside lamp and placed it inside of the car that the trailer was hitched up to, making sure the Egyptian figurine-based lamp would be safe and out of harm's way.

The lady then waved goodbye and got inside of the car. Juanita was still waving goodbye long after the woman's hand had dropped out of sight. I figured she was now waving bye-bye to the last of her furnishings, the last remnants of her past.

Sold and gone were all the material things she'd once valued as much as her pride and dreams. The Dolce & Cabana dresses and sexy evening wear. The Prada, Yves Saint Laurent to the Cardin and the Victoria's Secrets. The old Tommy Girl casual but expensive outfits. The leather and suede minis. The minks and other furs. The gator shoes, boots, bags and accessories. The shine, the ice, necklaces, watches and rings. The flat screen tele-vision. The Gucci-printed sofa and loveseats. The china and gold silverware. Everything. Even the Viper was replaced by a used Toyota Cressida.

"Well," she exhaled, "that's the last of it."

We walked back inside of the house and its emptiness made the house look huge. Only the refrigerator, stove and microwave remained in the kitchen.

Juanita tidied up as she went from room to room making sure the house wouldn't be left a mess when she turned it over to the new owners tomorrow.

The sun had gone down when she finished cleaning the place. A little exhausted and a bit sad, she sat down on the floor pillow next to me. I held her in my arms, neither of us speaking for a very long while.

"You hungry?" she asked, breaking the silence.

I nodded.

I can't even remember what she mixed up in the blender for me that night. I do recall that we were both tired and dozing off.

Not really saying much of anything. Our silence carried the moment. Juanita was still waiting on my decision. I hadn't yet told her she'd be leaving ATL without me. She'd asked me for my decision several times in the past few days. Each time I'd said I wouldn't make up my mind 'till the last minute. Maybe, deep down I was seriously considering leaving with her.

She sat up and placed her hand on my chest, under my sweatshirt. Her fingers traced the scars left from the old gunshot wounds.

"You're not leaving with me, are you?" Her voice was low, but strong. Knowing.

"I can't," I said. "I wish I could, but I can't."

She didn't say anything. She just got up and went into another part of the empty house.

I assumed Juanita was mad, so I let her be. I lay alone on the pillow in the center of the den's floor, wishing I was two people. One of me would stay in Atlanta and rule the streets. The other me would go with Juanita and try my hand at living legit.

Although she was gone, the smell of her Chanel perfume lingered on the pillow.

Damn! I'm trippin'.

Since when did a thug, robber and a killer get caught up in emotions? It tripped me out but then I started thinking about Shan and what caring about her had taught me: *Never love them hos!*

I never loved Cheryl. Inez, I liked a lot, but didn't love. Couldn't love her. Didn't know how.

24

Juanita was now standing over me, wrapped in only a towel. She went over to the fireplace and turned up the flame. When she returned to me, she sat down on the pillow, and I caught a glimpse of her auburn bush.

She said, "I haven't slept with anyone in months, and I'm not doing this to try to change your mind. I'm doing it because I'm scared I'll never see you again once I leave. If I don't, I'll always remember this night. If there's any such thing as fate, tonight will bring us back together."

She kissed my closed lips and began undressing me.

I stood up, removing my jeans and boxers, tossing them on top of my shoes and shirt.

Juanita stood up and removed the towel.

"Be gentle with me," she whispered. "I'm not that big."

I've had my share of women and sexual escapades but nothing could ever equal up to the thug passion I shared with Juanita that night.

We didn't make love over and over again, all night long. In fact, we only did it once, then fell asleep holding each other. But the shit was right, and it was something more than sex. There was silent crying coming from somewhere deep down inside of her as she held on to me, and I felt the wetness of her tears on my shoulder.

I wanted to tell her I'd leave with her, just up and say, "*Fuck the streets!*" But deep down I didn't believe I could succeed at anything else. I didn't know how to make *it* happen, unless *it* was with my heater.

Juanita was running away from the very thing that I loved and craved, the streets. We just weren't meant to be, I convinced myself that night.

The morning brought its ugly ass around too goddamn soon.

I watched Juanita pack her few remaining personal belongings into a single suit case. A dozen, or so, pairs of matching plain panties and bras, socks and toiletries. A few sweaters and a pair of jeans. A battered photo album and a folder with the words *Supreme Mathematics and Alphabets* written across it. She closed and locked the suitcase, and I picked it up to carry it out to the car for her.

She was carrying the teddy bear I'd given her the first time she'd invited me to her house for lunch. She locked the front door and dropped the door key inside a locked box that sat on the porch.

She had on old faded jeans and a baggy sweater that was covered by a patched jean jacket. Her hair was in a simple ponytail and she wore no makeup or lipstick. Juanita was definitely leaving the past behind.

Still, she looked beautiful, sexy and divine.

She kissed me on the lips and I tasted her tears.

"I'm not good at saying goodbye," she cried. Then she handed me a small gift bag.

"If you ever wish to find me, my mother will know how to contact me," Juanita sniffled.

I watched her get in the used Cressida and drive away to a new life. I got inside my whip, started the engine and I opened the gift bag Juanita had just given me. Inside was five thousand in cash, with a Jill Scott CD, the single, *Do You Remember Me?*

CHAPTER 4

I was hunting for that white bitch, Blondie, and her nigga night and day. Casing out the burned down sports bar, in case Little Gotti had to meet there with insurance agents, and the strip club where I'd first saw the white tramp.

I also kept tabs on Cheryl's mother. A few times a week I'd steal the mail out of her mailbox, thinking Cheryl might slip-up and write or send a postcard. But after three months of fruitless searches, I cut back to stealing her mail once a week.

Glen had been easy to find. Matter of fact, he would've already been dead but I was letting time pass so when I *did* him, my sister, Toi, wouldn't automatically suspect me.

Lonnie was being the true nigga I knew him to be, riding shotgun on every turn. We had touched a nigga from the Westside for a little flow, but nothing a nigga could retire or live long on.

Inez was back staying at her crib, back pushing 'dro. We were still tight like thieves, trying to stack cheddar in our separate hustles. My seed was beginning to push her stomach out, but she was still looking fly. I looked forward to our baby coming into the world but I wasn't neglecting my seeds that were already here, especially my lil' man.

I had gone by Poochie's crib when she called to let me know Shan had dropped Lil' T off over there. He'd asked me why I couldn't open my mouth, and I'd told him the truth, "I got caught slippin'."

Fuck it. I wasn't gon' lie to my lil' man.

He said, "My mama's boyfriend, Pete, said you got beat up." Yeah, Pete would put it out there like that.

I had whipped through Englewood looking for Murder Mike a week ago and learned he was out of town, so I had no reason to hang around. I felt like niggaz were looking down on me. But, then again, maybe I was just trippin'. Mafuckaz knew I wasn't a pussy!

I ran into an old head from the hood and he told me that the streets were saying a bitch had run off with two hundred grand of mine. I had to laugh at that. Shit! The streets didn't know the half! I *wish* Cheryl had only dipped with two hundred grand. I'd still be sitting on eight and some change.

Murder Mike paged me and asked to meet him in Englewood, in the horseshoe. I told him I was tied up at the clinic, but I could get with him by seven o'clock. He said that was a bet.

When I pulled into the horseshoe and parked, it was past seven and dark outside. Not many niggaz were used to seeing the Nissan. The young dope slangers eyed the car with suspicion, trying to figure out whether I was Five-0, or somebody looking to buy crack or someone looking to do something more ominous, robbery perhaps.

A brave heart approached the Nissan.

"I got those double-up sacks. The—oh! Youngblood!" he shrieked after recognizing me. "Damn, nigga!" he asked. "You rollin' on the creep tip?"

I asked him if he'd seen Murder Mike but before he could come up with a reply, I saw Murder's black Navigator whip up. I got out of the Nissan and walked over to where Murder Mike was parked. He was talking to a couple of his workers who stood a foot from his truck listening attentively.

"If them suckaz want drama, give it to 'em!" I heard him tell the boys, who nodded and walked away, ready to do just that.

Murder Mike was opening his door to get out of the truck when he saw me. "Whud up, main man?" he beamed our customary greeting. "Hop in, we need to rap."

I walked around to the passenger door and climbed in. He honked his horn at his workers and drove off.

Murder Mike said we were headed to one of his cribs in Lithonia to talk. He said *one of* like he had several cribs.

Damn! Main man must be stronger than the streets realized.

I left the thought silent as we drove east on I-20. I was guessing that Murder Mike had found out who had banged me up, and we were headed to *one* of his houses to discuss what I wanted to do about it. Or maybe he just wanted to show off his crib?

It was all good. Murder was my dawg. My main man from the hood.

The inside of the house was barely furnished, just a couch and big plasma television in the front room. The windows were covered with dark colored sheets, not curtains. Either Murder was just moving in or it was a stash house.

When we got to the kitchen and he turned on the light, I saw that I was right. Ten kilos were stacked on the counter and another five were on the kitchen table surrounded by a pile of crack cookies.

Murder took the kilos off the table and put them on the counter with the others. He put the crack inside large Ziploc bags and stacked them in a cardboard box on top of the refrigerator. He pulled another box down from atop the refrigerator and dumped its contents out on the table, revealing a huge pile of loose bills, of varying denominations and a bag of assorted color rubber bands.

"Have a seat, main man," he said, sitting down across from me. He began separating the pile of money into thousand-dollar stacks, mixing the denominations at random.

I was packing heat, but the thought of jacking Murder Mike never entered my mind. Just like Lonnie was my tightman, my partner in crime, Murder was my main man, my nigga, my dawg.

We were the same age, give or take a couple of months, and had grown up in Englewood playing everything together from stickball to truth-or-dare, elevating to stealing out of stores to stealing cars. I'd gotten caught a few times and was sent to YDC. Murder had gotten caught once and switched over to slangin' rocks. We didn't hang together when I came home from juvie, or even later, because he was always in the trap, on the grind. While I was out to get mine much faster, the ski mask way.

Still, the love and respect was mutual. We were just doing our own things.

Even though I was no longer sitting on grownup money, with my heater just a reach away, I wasn't tempted to take what he had just exposed to me.

He said, "Main man, I'm about to do major things. If shit goes as planned, the city is mine! I'ma take over the whole mafucka, whoady!" He paused. I guess he was giving his words time to register with me as he was still counting thousand dollar stacks. But I was silent, listening.

Murder claimed to have people behind him that were *dead serious* about taking over the drug game, and not only in the ATL. He was talking big, like some coast-to-coast shit. The plan, he said, was for him to start in Atlanta while his people would be doing the same in other major cities spaced out all the way to the West Coast.

"I want you on my team, main man," he said.

I replied, "I wish you luck, dawg, but you know selling dope ain't my expertise."

"Naw, nigga." Murder laughed, "You got the game twisted. I ain't talking about putting you in no trap or even having you driving dope from here to there. I want you to be my right hand, my eyes in the back of my head. Oversee everything I put together."

I was listening. My interest was piqued.

"You know," Murder continued, "for *us* to rise, other niggaz gotta fall. We gotta take 'em out the game. I know you ain't scared to get a body, nigga."

I smiled. He didn't know the half.

Then he started naming mafuckaz we'd have to take off the shelf. Some of them I didn't know. Some I knew well.

"The first head to roll is Rich Kid's," he said. I knew he was challenging me. "His time is up! I'm the new kid on the block!"

Rich Kid was major and I questioned whether Murder Mike had the guns to go to war against him or the guile to catch Rich Kid slippin'.

"Yeah, well, Hannibal *was* major, too," he reminded me. "Still, him and his right hand man turned up floating face-down in a lake."

As I was recalling reading about the incident months ago, he flashed his right hand inches from my eyes, the two platinum fingernails making his point loud and clear. Murder Mike had somehow caught Hannibal and his man slippin' and took 'em off the map. His point: *Rich Kid could be gotten, too.*

Platinum nails stood for bodies with Murder Mike.

He said, "I know you say you're not down with Rich Kid, but if you are, you're on the losing team."

Like a well-rehearsed play, four dreadlock-wearing mafuckaz came into the kitchen and surrounded the table, each of them packing sawed-offs. Murder didn't flinch or stop counting and separating the pile of money, so I knew it wasn't a stickup. They had to be part of his team.

I looked to my right and saw the big Dread who'd thrown me inside of the van and had delivered most of the punishment to my jaw and ribs. To my left was the one who'd scooped up my burner and had helped toss me out the moving van. Next to him was a real skinny, pocked-faced Dread. Directly in front of me, and at

Murder's side, was the mafucka who'd pointed the sawed-off at me from inside of the van.

Again, he had a shotgun pointed squarely at my chest. Once again he barked, "Don't be stoopid, mon!"

I looked across the table at Murder Mike, my main man. My nigga. My dawg. I couldn't believe it! I had never even suspected him. It didn't make sense, but now I understood. He hadn't believed me when I'd told him I wasn't pushing weight for Rich Kid. He'd also been in Englewood the night the Dreads had snatched me up from outside the music store. It was he who'd let them know when I had left the horseshoe. Perhaps they'd been waiting somewhere close by. He would have known I was holding down Inez and where she lived.

He was smiling at me from across the table. "It was business, main man," he said. "Nothing personal."

My hand was itching. I wanted to reach for my heater so mafuckin' bad! *How wasn't it personal when he had ordered me to get banged up? Or at least went along with the plan?* I was so mad, my face started twitching.

Don't be stoopid, mon! kept reverberating in my mind.

I knew the odds were against me. It would've been nearly impossible to pull my burner and kill four crazy, shotgun packing Dreads *and* Murder Mike, without getting slumped myself. This wasn't a Hollywood movie. This shit was real! And Murder must've known I wouldn't try to buck on those odds, which was probably why he hadn't bothered to search me for a weapon.

I was mad as hell, but I had to respect his gangsta. Now things made sense to me, even his strong bond with Cita.

I recalled that Cita had an aunt who was married to a Dread. If my memory was correct, it was the Dread with the pocked-marked face. I'd seen them together once.

"So what you say, mon? You join da winning team?" the big Dread asked. Like I was stupid enough to say *no* and get splattered all over the kitchen walls.

"I'm down," I said because a different answer would've ended my life. I was just buying some time.

Murder smiled platinum, then reached across the table to dap hands with me. "I know you stay strapped, main man," he said all of sudden. "Let me put your gun up until you calm down and hear the rest of our plans."

Yeah, nigga, you bet' not slip! I thought.

Four shotguns remained trained on me until Murder Mike picked my heater up off of the table, where I'd just placed it. I stood up and lifted my sweat shirt, proving to them that I wasn't packing more heat. Still the big Dread patted me down.

Murder clasped his hands together behind his head. I focused on his short dreadlocks and leaned back in his chair.

"Sorry about that lil' beat down. They weren't gonna kill you, though. I told them you're my dawg, and we could use you on our team," he explained.

One of the Dreads had fired up some ganja and passed it to me. I put the fat joint to my lips and sucked in the smoke through my teeth. I hit the joint a few times and passed it to Murder, who shook his head *no*, so I passed it back to the Dread who'd passed it to me.

The big Dread was called Rastaman. The one who'd scooped up my burner the night they'd snatched me was called Jamaican Rick. Cita's aunt's husband, the Dread with the pocked-marks, was Rohan, and the one I interpreted as the leader was called Crazy Nine.

Now that I knew who banged me up, I was no longer worried about the enemy kicking in Inez' door and bringing the ruckus. I had told them I was down with their team, and I couldn't see a way to reverse my decision. They knew where I laid my head, while all I knew was where one of Murder's stash houses were at and that he had workers in Englewood.

I could warn Rich Kid that they were about to come after him, join teams with him and go after them, but I was no longer sure how to read Rich Kid after what my sister had told me.

Glen had caught Toi with Rich Kid twice. Once having dinner at a restaurant and the second time getting out of Rich Kid's car in the parking lot of her condo.

Rich Kid had been fucking my sister all along, had even known why Glen had jumped on her. Yet he'd left me in the blind. The day he'd taken me to the hospital to pick up Toi, he'd acted like nothing had ever existed between my sister and him. They had played me for a fool!

Did that mean I couldn't trust Rich Kid? I wasn't sure. It certainly meant he wasn't on the up-and-up with me. Why hadn't he checked Glen for beating up my sister? His indifference showed that he thought my sister was just another bitch. If my peeps was just another bitch to him, then I couldn't be more than just another nigga. 'Cause if he had respect for me, it should've extended to my blood, Toi.

Yet, Rich Kid had always played fair with me concerning business. I wasn't sure I could take him off the shelf just 'cause he'd been fucking my sister without telling me. On the other hand, I'd have to do Murder Mike if I didn't slump Rich Kid. Or I could go wherever Juanita had gone to escape from the streets. But that would be like tucking my tail and running. I'm a dog, not a mutt!

I wanted to holla at Lonnie and see what he thought of my options, but Murder Mike had made it clear that he didn't trust Lonnie. He didn't want him in his business. He said that he had a gut feeling that Lonnie wasn't as solid as niggaz thought. I hadn't debated with him about it, but I couldn't think of another nigga in the world who felt that way about my tightman. Lonnie had never shown me any sign that he wasn't the solid nigga he claimed to be. Like me, he was a stickup kid, but he never targeted those he swore loyalty to. Nor did he have loose lips.

My dilemma was real 'cause I'd sworn loyalty to Rich Kid. At least, I sort of implied it when I told him I never did *work* against those I'd done *work* for. That was the code I lived by and Murder Mike was asking me to break it. But how real would I be if I didn't honor the codes I believed in? I'd be no better than Shotgun Pete, who let pussy make him violate the code between partners, an unspoken code that was supposed to be respected.

The only question was whether Rich Kid had surrendered his immunity from my gun when he started fucking my sister and keeping me blind to it.

Toi wasn't hands off but out of respect for me, Rich Kid should've respected her. He wasn't respecting her by fucking her behind her man's back, like she was nothing more than a jump off. The same way I treated hos like Fiona. He couldn't have love for my sister if he knew her nigga had fractured her jaw and he didn't do nothing about it. In fact, he sat back and let me go out on the limb over some shit he helped create.

Why should I have more concern for his welfare than he had for Toi's? Or was I just looking for justification to go along with Murder's plan?

The plan was for me to hit Rich Kid on a certain day, at a specific time. At the same time, Murder's Englewood crew would be hitting Rich Kid's peeps, who worked by the basketball court in Englewood, while the Dreads would be down in Fort Lauderdale, Florida, hitting Rich Kid's Cuban supplier.

Murder even knew about Rich Kid's Kentucky crew, who were regulating their hood since King's demise. A plan was devised to have them blasted at the same time the other hits were taking place.

Murder was taking a crew up to Kentucky himself. He told me, "Main man, it's gonna be just like that Saint Valentine's Day Massacre shit that the mob pulled off!"

The stakes were definitely sky high.

Deep down, though, I wanted to warn Rich Kid. I just liked the nigga. I simply had to decide what my next move would be after I warned him.

As fate would have it, a week later I ran into Rich Kid at a car wash on Moreland Avenue, up the street from the game room. He was in a sparkling new Chevy SS truck with big chrome rims and small TV screens built into the rear bumper. Not only was niggaz fawning over the truck, they were sweatin' the hell out of the chick with Rich Kid.

Straight up, shawdy had a face like a young Vivica Fox, a small waist and an ass like Buffy the Body. How she got all that booty inside those Baby Phat jeans she was wearing was a mystery to me.

Rich Kid saw me pull up in my truck. He left his eye candy leaning against his whip and came over to where I'd parked.

"What's up, fam'?" he asked, giving me dap.

"I'm good."

We both leaned on the hood of my trunk.

I gotta tell big homey how it's 'bout to go down. Fuck Murder Mike and 'em, tryna force my hand and shit.

I was still peeved that Rich Kid hadn't come clean about him and Toi, but my code of loyalty was weighing on me.

Maybe he does have some love and respect for my sister but didn't want to get caught up in no shit with her nigga, I considered, for the sake of giving him the benefit of the doubt.

"You a'ight, ain't you? Rich Kid asked. I guess he could tell that something was on my mind.

I was about to tell him that he was livin' on borrowed time unless we hooked up and rode on Murder Mike and his clique first 'cause they would definitely be gunnin' for him real soon, but for some reason I just said, "I'm a'ight, playboy. Other than my shit being wired up. But I'ma straighten that in a lil' bit. Anyway, those TV screens in the bumper of your SS is some real fly shit."

"Yeah, niggaz ain't ready fa dat," he smiled.

"Shawdy you're with is fly, too. Look at all them niggaz sweatin' her over there."

"Yeah, that ho thick wit' it, ain't she?"

"Thick to death! But then that's how you roll. Straight up, she's the finest I've seen you with yet. You might wanna wife that one."

"Wife her?" Rich Kid asked, looking at me like I had said something about his mama. "Man, I wouldn't wife that bitch if she came with a ten-million-dollar inheritance. Anyway, the ho already married. I'm just dickin' her on the side."

"Well, her nigga must be pussy 'cause you ridin' lil' mama around like it's all good. What if her man was to ride up on y'all?"

"Shid, that'll be shawdy's problem. He could snatch her outta my truck and kick the ho's ass all up and down Moreland for all I care. Just as long as the nigga don't get fly out the mouth with *me.*"

"You wouldn't even check the nigga?" I forced a laugh.

"Check him for what? Any ho who fucks behind her man's back deserves a beat down. I ain't got love for a ho who'll creep." *So that's how you felt about my sister, huh?* I thought. "I feel you, playa," I replied halfheartedly.

Later that day, I called Toi.

As soon as she answered the phone I said, "I just want you to know while you was creepin' around with that nigga Rich Kid, causing Glen to fuck you up and causing me to wet him up, Rich Kid ain't give a fuck about you."

"I figured that out when he didn't even offer to step to Glen," Toi acknowledged. "That's why I told him to fuck off when he called asking to hook up again."

"Oh, he tried to holla again *after* you got out of the hospital?"

"Yep."

Grimey ass nigga! I thought. *Nigga tryna treat my peeps like a straight ho!*

"Anyway, why you bring all that back up after all this time?" Toi asked.

"No reason. I'ma holla later."

I hung up the pay phone, hopped in my whip, pushed in a Scarface CD and drove around the city with some heavy shit on my mind. I had one helluva decision to make.

For the next few days, my son came to stay at Inez' crib with us. I was spending time with him and Inez in case my decision meant I wouldn't see them for a while. My mood was kind of sullen, and Inez commented on it more than once.

My mood improved the day before I took Lil' T back to Shan, and I got the wire taken out of my jaw. I was trying to make up for lost time I hadn't spent with him over the past months.

After I took Lil' T home, I bought some pizza and went back to Inez'. It had been months since I'd been able to eat solid food, so I pigged out so much my jaws hurt. But they didn't hurt too bad to stop me from doing another thing I hadn't done in a while.

I told Inez to go take a bath and then wait for me naked on the bed. When I entered the bedroom with a can of whipped cream, she knew it was on.

Ca$h

CHAPTER 5

My watch read 8:15 p.m. Rich Kid had agreed to meet me outside the game room at nine. I'd talked to him earlier in the day, explaining that I needed to see him ASAP. He pressed me on why it was so urgent, even though we both knew it was always unwise to discuss business over the phone.

I'd said as much as I dared say on a phone, telling him that shit had been a little rough for me since I got out the hospital, and I needed him to loan me some loot so Inez and I could go out of town until I dealt with my enemies.

"Do I know the nigga you got beef with?" he asked.

"Maybe," I said. "But I'ma handle it. I just want Inez out of town, somewhere safe, while I do."

"It's that serious, huh?" Rich Kid asked.

I said, "It is with me! You saw how fucked up I was!"

He asked if I was okay. We hadn't seen each other since the day at the car wash.

"I'm good," I assured him. "Just ready to handle my biz and get back to flossin' on mafuckaz."

He asked how much loot I wanted to borrow.

I told him, and he replied, "No problem. I'll meet you outside the game room at eight tonight?"

"Can we make it nine?" Which would be better for me.

"Yeah," he agreed. "Nine is cool."

We hung up.

Spring had just kicked in, so it was still a little cool at night. I wore jeans, a pullover Braves sweatshirt, a Braves fitted cap and black Timbs.

I dropped Inez off at her Ma Duke's crib to spend time with her daughter and then stopped at a BP gas station to put gas in the Nissan.

By the time I reached the game room, it was 8:45, so I just sat in the car and waited. I was changing CDs when Rich Kid drove up in his Chevy SS. I flashed my headlights at him and he stopped about two car lengths ahead of me. I got out so he'd see me, not sure if he'd recognize my Nissan since I rarely drove it. He did recognize me, though, and he pulled into a parking space several cars down from where I was parked. I'd noticed a female in the passenger seat of his whip. It looked like the same shawdy from the car wash.

By the time I walked up to where he was parked, Rich Kid was already outside of the car leaning against the side of it. I stopped about three feet in front of him, raised my arm and squeezed the trigger of the .9mm in my hand.

Splacka! Splacka! Splacka! Splacka! Splacka!

The nine spat automatic gun-fire. All to his chest! I watched him slide down the side of the Benz, smoke coming from the front of his shirt. The bitch jumped out the whip, running and screaming. I hopped over Rich Kid and ran her down.

Splacka! Splacka! Two straight to the dome.

I pulled the fitted cap down low over my brow. A few people were in the parking lot, staring in horror, then scrambling to get out of my way. I held my head down so they couldn't see my face, dashed to the Nissan and drove off quickly, without squealing the tires.

I felt safe when I made it to the Interstate and blended in with night traffic.

Ten miles down the expressway, a car pulled alongside me honking its horn, the driver waving his free arm frantically. I rolled down my window, gripping Nina.

"Hey, buddy!" the white man shouted out of his window as he tried to steer straight. "You're missing your tags!"

"Thanks!" I yelled back and then eased up off my .9mm.

Of course I was missing my license plate. I had removed it when I stopped to get gas.

I drove on to Inez' and put the tag back on the Nissan before going inside.

A few days later, I traded it in and bought a newer model. I was just taking the necessary precautions.

The streets were hot with rumor and gossip, especially down in Englewood where several of Rich Kid's crew had gotten splacked the same night, same time that he had. The hood had no way of knowing about the successful hits in Florida and Kentucky, but Murder and the four Dreads were back in Atlanta acting awfully satisfied with themselves.

I was watching the news daily to see if the police were any closer to identifying the gunman outside the game room. Witnesses had correctly described the Nissan and were fairly accurate on my height and weight, but they'd incorrectly described the gunman as having short cut hair and couldn't give any details on the gunman's complexion.

The Nissan was no longer in my possession. Besides, witnesses hadn't been able to report any tag number. Still I was keeping a low profile.

The bitch I'd splacked had died on the scene, the news reported. But Thaddeus Brown, A.K.A. Rich Kid, was still clinging to life, despite five slugs to the chest and abdomen.

Damn! I should've shot him in the head! I admonished myself, though I was sure he wouldn't pull through and survive. I was just hoping he didn't wake up long enough to identify his assailant.

Murder and the Dreads weren't upset about it.

"If he lives, you'll just have to find a way to finish the job," they said.

I was all for that 'cause I didn't want Rich Kid walking around with my name on a hit list, no way. He'd lost a couple of soldiers in the Englewood battle also. If he did survive, he'd find that his Cuban supplier was missing and his Kentucky crew had suffered their own tragedies.

I moved out of the Decatur apartment into a townhouse south of the city and told Inez to start looking for a new spot, too. Murder Mike broke me off some cash flow but said we had other people to eliminate before we could put the operation into top gear.

While the Dreads went to different cities across the country to continue setting up their respective zones, Murder Mike and I stayed posted in Atlanta. We were together more than we were apart over the next few months, plotting our mission.

Murder showed me the hit list with the names of all those we were to eliminate.

The list read:
Hannibal (X) plus his LT.
Rich Kid (?)
Little Gotti
LA Steve
BCF
José

I guess the X next to Hannibal's name signified he'd already been eliminated. The ? next to Rich Kid's name would become an X once he expired.

My main man didn't have to tell me anything but where to find Little Gotti and when he wanted the nigga hit. Blondie would be personal.

LA Steve was a nigga I didn't know, but Murder had the 411 on him.

He said, "Dude doesn't fuck with cocaine, his steelo is weed. Most of the 'dro and skunk weed in the city comes from him. If we get rid of LA Steve, we can lockdown the weed game, too. More mafuckaz smoking weed than crack nowadays."

"Bet," I agreed.

BCF, which stood for Black Crime Family, was a drug clique out of Detroit that had recently came to ATL and setup shop. Besides pumping drugs, they were strong in the music industry. I didn't really know much about BCF, but I'd seen their billboards around the city, promoting their record label, Street Life Productions. Their rep was bubbling in the streets.

As for José, the last name on Murder's hit list, he was a big time Mexican nigga with a team of trigger happy *ese's*.

"They're deep out there in Gwinnet County," Murder Mike informed me.

I have to say, I was mad impressed with the wealth of information my man, Murder, had on all these players in the game. Though I suspected the Dread, Crazy Nine, had supplied most of it.

Still, until recently I would've never thought Murder Mike possessed anything more than street-level skills in the dope game. The same hustle skills the average nigga from the hood possessed—no plans beyond locking down his block. Now I had to look at my main man with much more respect. He was after more than hood fame and lil' boy money.

I was still a little peeved about him siccing the Dreads on me like he did, even if I did understand the business sense of it. Murder had since told me that he'd told them before they'd grabbed me, if they killed me, they'd have to kill him, too.

"Main man," he'd said, sounding real, "I was pissed when I found out your jaw was broken! It wasn't supposed to go like that! But that fool, Rastaman, don't know his own power."

I had interrupted him. "They were beating me with lead pipes, I don't know how it *wouldn't* go like it did."

He swore that he hadn't been told anything, beforehand, about lead pipes and shit.

"I put that on everything I love, dawg. Shit," he said, "it wasn't even my call that you get roughed up. I told Crazy that I took your word for it that you weren't on Rich Kid's team."

"That's on all you love?" I asked, staring him in the eyes.

He didn't blink. "For sho'! Look, I felt I could step to you and get you to roll with us, without all the drama. We do go way back."

So I accepted Murder Mike's explanation and apology because it made sense to me. Why would he want me banged up? He probably would have talked me into joining up with him and the Dreads without resorting to putting me in the hospital. He said that he also figured that was Crazy Nine's way of intimidating me, so if I did join the team, I'd never get the dumb idea to rob them.

"That *was* your steelo, homeboy," Murder said.

I accepted it all in stride, not letting it affect what I felt for Murder Mike. But it's hard to like a mafucka who put you in the hospital with a broken jaw and cracked ribs. So while I would get money with Murder Mike and the Dreads, my loyalty was to him only.

To be honest, though, I didn't feel good about splackin' Rich Kid. I wasn't sure if I'd done it because the Dreads had me boxed in, or if I'd done it because Cheryl had run off with my loot and it was a chance for me to get down with Murder Mike and 'em and get my bank back tight. Or if I'd really done it because Rich Kid hadn't shown any respect or loyalty to me or Toi. What really got Rich Kid wet the fuck up was that shit he popped at the car wash. It felt like he was referring to Toi, too.

46

Either or, what was done was done. I couldn't take back the five slugs I'd pumped in Rich Kid. Wasn't no erasing that. I had chosen sides and there was no turning back.

For all of my young years, I'd wanted no real part of the drug game, other than robbing dope boys. Now I was part of a drug crew that was both deadly and ambitious!

Once we had control of the city's drug flow, my role would be mostly that of an enforcer and an overseer. I wouldn't be able to replace the million dollars Cheryl stole overnight, but I wouldn't have to scout out licks no more, either.

It took a few weeks for me to reconcile with my change of *professions*, but it wasn't too difficult to do because until we eliminated those on the hit list, most of my work would involve using my heater.

That was a role I was very used to.

Ca$h

CHAPTER 6

The first person I hit with Murder Mike was the nigga known in the streets as LA Steve, the major weed supplier in the city.

We had tracked his movements for nearly two weeks, not always following him, but always aware of where he'd be during certain times of the night.

Everyone had a routine. Some people were more structured than others, but none are impossible to chart. Routine was what we were used to doing, what we grow comfortable with. Niggaz got uncomfortable when something upsetted their routine. So when I was casing-out my victims, I began with a simple theory that's usually reliable: *If a nigga goes to a certain place once, he'll eventually go back there again. If he goes there twice or more, well, that's basis to figure out his routine.*

I didn't need to know where he'd be every minute of the day, not even every day of the week. All I really needed to know was *when* he'd be at the place where I planned to hit him.

Even *I* had a certain routine. If a nigga knew where Inez lived, and wanted to hit me, all he had to do was wait for me to show up at her crib and I was a dead man!

LA Steve was no different, only we didn't know who his woman was or where she lived. His undoing was his love of shrimp. Funny how such a simple thing as a man's favorite food could set him up to be murdered. But in LA Steve's case it did.

For two consecutive Thursday nights, he'd gone to the All-You-Can-Eat Shrimp special offered at The Seafood House on Fulton Industrial Highway.

Both times, he'd arrived between 7 and 10 p.m. Once, he'd been alone. The other time, he'd taken along a woman. Which didn't matter to Murder Mike, me or our heaters. Neither of us discriminated against women. I didn't get no special kick out of

49

killing hos, but neither did I love killing niggaz. I was indifferent to both, it was just business.

On the third Thursday, we waited 'til 11 p.m. for LA Steve to show up at The Seafood House. At midnight the restaurant closed without him showing his face. Either he was tired of shrimp on Thursdays or something else had kept him away.

A few days later, Murder Mike learned that a big load of hydro weed had just touched down in the city. It was safe to assume LA Steve had gone out of town to pick it up. That would explain why he hadn't made his Thursday appointment at The Seafood House last week.

I betted Murder Mike a thousand dollars LA Steve would not miss the All-You-Can-Eat Shrimp special next Thursday night.

Thursday Night 9:05 p.m.

We watched from the doughnut shop's parking lot, across the street, as a green Range Rover pulled into an empty parking space toward the rear of The Seafood House. Murder Mike handed me a roll of rubber band-wrapped bills and I put the wad in the pocket of the jumpsuit with the thousand dollars I was carrying in case I had lost the bet.

"I hope the punk enjoys his last meal. It cost me a thousand dollars!" said Murder Mike, not really angry. He'd lost the bet, but he'd win the bigger prize.

LA Steve was alone when he walked inside of the restaurant to feast on the All-You-Can-Eat Shrimp special. We figured it would take him his usual forty-five minutes to enjoy his meal, so we rode off on a Ninja 1100, not wanting to be noticed waiting around.

Murder Mike and I were both wearing black leather racing suits. His was a little looser-fitting than mine, to allow room for the double-barrel sawed-off that was concealed down the front left side of it.

We rode around aimlessly for the next thirty minutes, just passing away idle time until I felt our target would have eaten his last shrimp. Then I headed back toward The Seafood House, stopping momentarily, a few blocks away, so that Murder Mike could turn around and straddle the bike seat backwards, his back to mine. We strapped a wide car seat-like belt around the both of us, effectively locking us together, back to back. If one of us fell off the bike, the other would fall with him. But the wide belt around us was necessary to give Murder more stability and balance in case both of his hands were still pre-occupied when we drove off after the hit.

LA Steve had a cell phone to his ear as he exited the restaurant, strolling casually toward his vehicle. I waited for him to get out of the view of the restaurant's side windows before I rode across the street. He turned around toward the loud sound of the Ninja, perhaps upset that the roar of the bike's engine was drowning out his phone conversation.

I slowed the bike as we drew even to our target and brought it to an almost complete stop three yards past him, so that Murder Mike was now facing LA Steve.

I heard the loud report of the double barrel sawed-off.

Boom! Boom!

The kickback from the weapon jarred Murder's back against mine. I hesitated just a few seconds before pulling off, to allow my accomplice time to put the sawed-off down the front of his racing suit, freeing his hands to hold onto the back of the bike's seat for added balance.

The Ninja zoomed down Fulton Industrial Highway like a blur. We merged onto I-285 and drove back to the stash house in Lithonia. There I guided the bike into the driveway and behind the house, where Murder Mike unlocked the belt that held us together.

We sat at the kitchen table, helmets at our elbows, congratulating each other on the professional job we'd just done. My adrenalin was sky high, while Murder Mike appeared his normal self.

I half-expected him to pull dope or money from the cabinet and go about business as usual. Instead he got up from the table into the back of the house. After a short while, he returned in jeans and a sweat shirt.

"I gotta run to the pay phone," he said. "I'll grab us something to eat while I'm out."

As soon as I heard his Navigator back out of the yard and drive off, I went back to the bathroom to take a leak and to make sure I was alone in the house. Just to satisfy my own curiosity, I made a quick inspection of every room in the house, careful to put things back in the order they were. I looked everywhere: closets, under beds, under sinks, cabinets, everywhere. No dope or money anywhere. Not that I would've taken it had I found any, I was just curious to know if my main man already trusted me enough to leave me alone at the house with the amounts of coke and money that had been there the last time. It didn't disappoint me not to find a stash there, I understood the rules of the streets, trust had to be earned.

The thing that was hardest for me to understand was why clap a nigga who was sitting on major figures without robbin' him also? The shit just didn't make sense to me. We were taking him off the shelf. Why not grab his loot in the process? Of course, it wasn't always easy to find a nigga's stash. The wiser dope boys didn't keep their stash where they laid their heads. Common sense said it was kept somewhere close by, easy to get to in a hurry.

Murder thought like the dope boy he was, not like a robber. His sole interest was in eliminating the competition, then he'd clock his own riches. I had to respect it since he was the one calling the shots. It was their operation, their ball to bounce. Still, I felt it was stupid not to rob mafuckaz before we crossed 'em off the hit list.

One name we couldn't cross of the hit list yet was Rich Kid's. Yep, the nigga survived five shots, fired from close range. Though he hadn't died, he was in no shape to mount revenge. Word was he had been flown by helicopter to a hospital in Maryland to undergo more surgery and then extensive therapy.

He wasn't an immediate threat to me, but I would still have to monitor his progress because I was absolutely sure he would seek revenge.

With Rich Kid convalescing in Maryland, his remaining soldiers in Englewood had no supplier, no dope to push. Murder immediately expanded his Englewood crew to more than a dozen workers, even posting half of them up by the basketball court where Rich Kid's crew used to regulate.

It didn't take a warfare expert to figure out that Murder Mike had been involved in the assault on Rich Kid and the hit on his crew, for he was the immediate and sole beneficiary of Rich Kid's demise.

A few of the young rollers who had slang dope for Rich Kid by the basketball court and had survived the assault by Murder's crew, tried to avenge the deaths of their two comrades who'd gone down in the Englewood shootout. They were unorganized and seriously outgunned and were little more than a nuisance to our boys now regulating the trap by the ball court. Still they had to be dealt with before one of their ill-planned drive-by's were successful and we lost a soldier or two.

The reckless lil' niggaz weren't hard to find. They were Englewood born, bred and raised and any number of their family members and girlfriends still lived there.

They'd creep back to visit late at night when the traps were closed, and our soldiers caught two of them doing just that. By the time the two reckless niggaz' girlfriends came out to investigate the late-night gunshots, the only person who could do anything for their boyfriends was the undertaker.

The hood caught heat from the cops for a week or two, but with no eye witnesses to the killings, po-po eventually returned to their regular routine.

Street niggaz were forced to respect Murder Mike's ambition and his crew's willingness to let their heaters bark. Englewood was now established as Murder Mike's turf.

Bit by bit, the plan was coming together, showing progress toward the ultimate goal of controlling the city's drug flow. I had no way of knowing how the Dreads were coming along in their respective cities across the US, but Murder told me they were progressing at least as well as we were in Atlanta.

CHAPTER 7

Though there was still much work to be done, occasionally we made time for play, if for no other reason than to break the monotony of murder and drug dealing. The game could eventually drain a nigga's energy and make him more susceptible to mistakes.

To his credit, Murder Mike understood that we all needed a break from the everyday grind.

Neither he nor I wanted to hang out at nightclubs and leave ourselves open to enemy attack, so I took Inez out to the house Murder and Cita stayed at in Austell, Georgia, by Six Flags amusement park.

The house was nice but not so extravagant to warrant suspicion as to how such a young couple could afford it.

The only vehicles I saw parked in the driveway were Cita's E-Class and the Navigator Murder had driven to meet us. The inside of the house was sparsely furnished, giving me the impression that they'd moved into the house recently. The backyard, where we barbequed, was spacious and well-kept.

Cita was dressed ghetto fabulous and hardly prepared to labor over a grill. Inez offered to help Murder Mike and before long the ribs, steaks and burgers were cooking over the hot charcoal.

Inez, in her seventh month of pregnancy, labored over the barbeque pit while Cita pretended to be a diva, too beautiful and high maintenance to get her hands dirty with sauce or the likes. The bitch was really just a glorified hood rat, along for the ride with a nigga who had his sights set on the top. If something was to befall Murder Mike, Cita's ghetto ass would be right back down in the hood happy to even *smell* barbeque.

All evening long she was acting superior, dropping hints that translated into: *Now that you work for my man, I'm better than you and your girl!*

Murder was trying to put her in check without making it obvious he had caught her innuendo. My nigga wasn't on no high horse just 'cause he was the shot caller. He knew that we still put our pants on the same way and I wasn't nobody's *do* boy. Once, he even called Cita in the house, like he needed her to help him find the Cristal, but I knew he was in there checking the bitch for her uppity attitude.

Ain't this the same bitch that was all on my dick a few months ago, every time Murder turned his head? Or was this payback for me stiff-arming the bitch and putting her on blast to my main man at the club that time?

Inez wasn't feelin' the bitch either, in fact, she had whispered to me that she was gonna check her. She planned to remind Cita that if she was truly a diva, her knees wouldn't be ashy as hell.

I laughed and told Inez to chill. We'd make it through the evening.

When we got back to the new spot Inez had moved into just last week, she had me cracking the fuck up by mimicking Cita.

"Some folks get a little money," she said, finishing with her impromptu performance of Cita, "and just don't know how to act. *Whew!*" Shaking her head. "I wanted to slap that bitch!"

"Murder Mike is cool, though," I offered.

"Yeah," Inez agreed, "he was pretty nice." She took off her shoes and showed me her beautiful but pregnant swollen feet. "Rub them for me," she purred.

"I will if you promise me some of that good pussy."

"Aw, nigga, you know you're getting some of this good stuff tonight!"

I massaged and rubbed her feet until she said it was time for her to deliver her end of the deal.

"I'm waiting." I laid back on the bed and pulled her on top of me.

"Baby, baby, baby," Inez muttered, like she couldn't wait to put that pussy on a nigga.

"Don't talk about it, *be* about it," I said.

"Oh, you ain't said nothing but a word," she replied as she began to slinky her way down my body and release my wood from its constraints.

The moment her mouth covered the head of my dick, all other things were temporarily forgotten. And when her sucking escalated to us fuckin', Inez riding me, I closed my eyes and allowed my shawdy to ease all of my worries.

***

The next day, the Navigator chewed up the highway but it could not distance itself from the drop top Benz. I could've whipped past Murder Mike anytime I chose to, but it would've been useless. I would've had to slow down and let him pass me, for he knew the way to Louisiana, and I didn't.

The city of New Orleans was famous for its jazz music, Mardi Gras, black colleges, crawfish, jambalaya, gumbo and, of course, witchcraft. None of which had enticed me to accompany Murder Mike to the city for a little fun, rest and relaxation.

I'd been baited into going to New Orleans by Murder's description of the beautiful Creole girls I'd get my choice of. I'd heard about Creole women, their beauty and passion, but I'd never seen or met one.

"You're gonna meet my real family, dawg," he said.

"I thought your family was your Ma Duke and 'em in Englewood?"

"Yeah, those are my real peeps," he confirmed. "But I'm talking about my own branch of the family tree, my wife and kids."

"Boy, stop!" I chuckled. "Yo' ass ain't married to nobody unless it's Cita!"

He said, with a straight face, "Naw, main man, Cita ain't nothing but my link to business, my bitch on the side. You'll meet my boo when we get to New Orleans."

"Your boo? Nigga, stop fronting." I laughed. "Cita is mufuckin' boo."

"Nah, family. I got a wife. Real shit."

The look on his face told me he was dead serious. Out of curiosity, I pressed him for details.

According to Murder, he'd met his wife, a Creole named Francisca, when she came to Atlanta to visit family a few years ago. Now they had a set of three-year-old twins and had been married for two years.

I was anxious to get to New Orleans. The city Master P had put on the rap map. A city being represented by The Cash Money Millionaires, Juvie and others.

After driving for hours, chopping it up about different things, we reached Francisca's house around noon.

As soon as Murder climbed out of the Navigator, his twins broke loose from their mother's grasp on the porch and raced into his arms. He bent to accommodate them, hoisting one up in each arm. The twins rained kisses all over his cheeks and talked in excited utterances. From my car in the driveway, I could see that Francisca was as pretty as a portrait, in an understated way.

"Boo, this is my partner, Youngblood," Murder introduced us as I carried my overnight bags inside. "Main man, this is my beautiful wife, Francisca."

"Hi. Pleased to meet you," she daintily shook my hand. "I'd prefer you call me Fran," she said.

Up close, Fran was still as pretty as she'd appeared from the driveway. Her hair was reddish brown, down to her butt in one thick braid. Her skin was the color of French ice cream, maybe a shade darker. She was petite but sexy, without trying to be. She wore no makeup, a sundress and a platinum set of wedding rings on the proper finger.

I knew from Murder Mike that Fran was twenty-four, but her voice sounded much younger, making her appear as delicate as a long stem rose. She called Murder Mike *Michael,* and he answered to his given name without complaint.

Immediately after our introduction, I showered and changed into long, baggy shorts and a long, loose fitting Mike Vick Jersey #7 emblazoned across the front and back, a studded black bandana wrapped around my forehead and braids. My Cuban link medallion replica of a coffin hung from my neck, both my wrists were iced and ankle-cut Timbs rocked my feet.

Fran's younger sister, Lolita, came over to the house with two of her girlfriends, one Spanish, the other black. The three of them were sophomores at Tulane University.

Lolita and the Spanish broad were eyeing me. The black girl was trying *not* to eye Murder, but I peeped her lose the battle more than once.

Lolita was a carbon copy of her sister, if I added a size to her titties, a few octaves to her voice and a little *hot* to her ass. She was definitely making sure I noticed her, but it was energy she could have saved.

Though she wasn't the finest of the bunch, I had come to New Orleans to taste the gumbo, the crawfish *and* a Creole. And she was the *only* Creole of the three.

Fran served us seafood and okra gumbo while we all sat around getting acquainted.

Watching *Michael* interact with Fran and the twins reminded me of how I used to act with Eryka and Chanté, like a big kid. It only further proved to me that no man, but a foolish one, was a gangster around his kids. It was obvious that Murder Mike had way more love and respect for Fran than he did for Cita. He didn't cuss around Fran or threaten to slap her lipstick crooked whenever her opinion differed from his.

In fact, I wondered if Fran knew what her Michael-poo's platinum fingernails represented? *Or did he keep her blind to that part of his life?* Regardless, she had to know that he wasn't a traveling salesman and that being married yet living in separate states was done for a reason.

She didn't strike me as dumb or gullible. She was a computer graphics designer for a major firm in New Orleans, so she wasn't being kept by my main man.

"We're going to the softball game at the park," Lolita announced. "Y'all want me to take the twins, so that y'all can have some time alone?" she asked Murder and Fran.

Like all kids, the twins got excited in a hurry, ready for the next car ride or adventure.

"Youngblood, you want to join us?" invited Lolita.

By the time we returned from the park, the twins were dirty and tired and there was no doubt as to whom I was interested in. We said goodbye to Lolita's college pals, Carmen and Iris. I grabbed some fresh gear and took it with me to Lolita's apartment where I was to shower, change and get ready to go with her to a club where Lil' Wayne was to perform.

Lolita's apartment was near the University. It was a small efficiency, about what you'd expect a college girl to stay in.

"We can shower together, to save time?" Lolita offered once we were inside and laying out the gear we'd rock.

I wasn't about to refuse that.

She let me get under the shower water first and lather up. Then I moved over to allow her to do the same. Lolita had known the shower stall was barely large enough for one person, let alone two. But she tried to be coy. But I was a million miles from being lame, so I wasn't buying her act. If the bitch didn't wanna get fucked, she would've never gotten into the shower with a nigga she'd known less than a day.

Soap suds stood up on her titties like snow on twin mountains. Water had already rinsed the suds from between her legs, revealing the neatest mass of reddish brown hair I'd ever seen covering a pussy. I could barely see her slit through the mass of silky red hair. She turned her back to me and I watched the water rinse suds down the crack of her tight ass. She turned around and saw my soap-sudded erection.

"What's this?" I felt her hand encircle me.

"That's Big Daddy!" I said.

She laughed. "Does Big Daddy mind if I give him a kiss," she purred in that southern Louisiana drawl.

"You can kiss him 'til your jaws hurt." I was all gangsta.

After a while, she came up for air and kissed me, but not with her tongue, just so that's clear and understood. She whispered in my ear, "You wanna return the favor?"

I picked her up and stepped out of the shower, both of us dripping wet. I laid her gently on the floor and then grabbed a towel, bunched it up and placed it under her ass so that her pussy stood up.

After I licked and sucked her into a frenzy, I mounted her and drove mad dick into her Creole pie. She panted like she was about to explode and I felt her warm juices flood.

61

She calmed down long enough to whisper in my ear, "Put it in the back door."

I wasn't about to refuse that, either.

I rubbed the head of my steel pole up and down her wet slit, lubricating it with her own juices and then I placed it on the hole of her brown cookie.

"Ooh! Go slow, baby," she moaned.

"I got you."

I took my time pushing further inside until I felt her body accept all of my length. Even then, I remained still while I kissed her on her neck and shoulders.

Lolita's breathing deepened and I felt her body thrust against mine. "Fuck my ass, daddy," she begged.

"That's what you want?"

"Hell yeah."

"Like this?" I pushed in and pulled out, quickening my rhythm with each stroke.

"Yessss! Just like that. Give me that dick!"

Her eagerness for me to fuck her ass had a nigga harder than ever. *I'm 'bout to punish this bitch.*

I drew out as far as I could and slammed back inside of her with force, repeatedly.

"Yes, baby! Fuck me until you bust all inside ass!" she cried.

"You like this shit? Huh? Tell me you like it!" I stroked deeper, while rubbing her clit furiously.

"I like it! I love it! I love it!" she screamed causing us both to erupt at the same time.

***

When we stepped out to go to the club, I was rockin' blue khakis, a Braves jersey, Braves fitted baseball cap, mad ice and my heater on my waist. Lolita had on a simple Tulane University sweat suit, a braided rope cross hung around her neck and lady Air Max 95's on her feet.

We whipped to the club with the top down on the Benz, T.I. blasting from the system. I'd put my heater in the secret compartment as soon as we'd left Lolita's spot, just in case po-po pulled me over, hatin' on a young nigga.

Traffic was bumper to bumper three blocks away from the club, and moving at a snail's pace.

New Orleans's hos were acting just like shawdies be acting in the ATL, yelling out of their cars at a nigga pushing a fly whip. *Damn the bitch with him!*

Whenever traffic crept to a standstill, one bitch or another would hop out of their car and shake her ass to the sounds booming out of niggas systems. Then the bitch would hop back in her ride and high-five her girlfriends. Lolita would laugh and comment that the girls were way bolder than her. I couldn't tell. Not after she'd asked for it in the ass a short while ago and took the dick like a champ.

I knew we'd never find an empty parking space close to the club's front door, so I just whipped up there to show off the drop. That way once I got inside of the club, hos would know that I was ridin' in style.

Luckily, I caught someone leaving a parking space not very far from the club's entrance. Before getting out the whip, I retrieved my heat from the hidden compartment.

"You can't take that inside the club!" Lolita warned me, sounding alarmed.

"Oh, they pat niggaz down?"

"Of course!"

I put the gun back.

"Check this, shawdy," I said seriously. "I don't wanna run into no trouble with one of your current or ex-boyfriends 'cause a nigga ain't with that petty drama. If I do run into it, I damn sho' don't wanna get caught without my shit."

She swore I wouldn't have to worry about that.

"My ex died from AIDS last week," she said.

"What?" I screamed.

She laughed. "I'm just kidding! My boyfriend is a professor at my school. He's married, and he most definitely won't be at a club like *this*."

Once inside, Lil' Wayne and the Big Tymers had the club jumpin'! New Orleans hustlers were representin' their spots, cliqued up and dimes on their jock.

I played the bar, sippin on Cognac, while Lolita got her party on. She wasn't my bitch and I wasn't a jealous nigga, so I told her to enjoy herself. She knew where to find me when it was time to bounce.

With her out of the way, I was free to choose other N'awlins hos. I couldn't help wondering, though, if Juanita wasn't somewhere at college, fuckin' her professor and taking it up the ass on the side. I doubted it, but still, I wondered where she was and what she was doing with her new life and all.

Hos didn't let me wonder for long, they interrupted my reverie within minutes of Lolita's departure. A hundred of them must've asked if I was from *Atlanter,* trying *not* to sound country but making the shit worse. What they didn't realize, obviously, was that I loved country hos.

I took a few phone numbers but spent the majority of the night 'versing with a slim goodie named Audrey, who told me she was Creole.

Lolita didn't seem to mind. I guess she understood I wasn't hers to claim. She was doing her thing anyway, partying, having a good time. Not really hoing, just shaking what her mama gave her.

Hours later, we left the club and went back to Fran's house to stay the night. I slept in the spare room, where I'd put my overnight bags. Lolita slept in the front room, on the couch, pretending she wasn't first night pussy.

The next morning after a breakfast of pancakes, eggs, and turkey bacon, I took Lolita home to her efficiency and retrieved the gear I'd left there.

Later, Murder and I went shopping at a big, fancy mall in a suburb of New Orleans. He copped several bags of gear, a platinum diamond and ruby bracelet and a thinner matching one for Cita. I copped a couple pair of Bugle Boy khakis, a jean jacket with a sewn-in picture of Louis Armstrong on the back, A New Orleans Saints sweatshirt for Lil' T, a few souvenirs for Inez, a postcard for Juanita, some shades for Lonnie and Apple Bottom jeans for Toi.

"You feelin' Lolita?" Murder asked while we were at the mall.

"Done felt her." I boasted.

"What?" He laughed.

"Yep," I reaffirmed. "It's a done deal, main man!"

He shook his head. "She's wild! Nothing like Francisca or their older sister, Consuella."

I told him I wasn't complaining, a nigga only lived once.

That evening, Lolita called over to Fran's house to tell me she might not get to see me again before I went back to Atlanta in a couple of days, but she hoped to see me the next time we came to N'awlins.

I wasn't used to a bitch hitting and running on me, but I complimented her on the Creole pie, anyway.

"We'll do it again," she promised.

I called up Audrey, the Creole shawdy from the club last night. She was glad to hear from a nigga so soon, and after following her directions, I was whippin' up in front of her apartment. I went inside to meet her grandmother, then we were off. She took me sightseeing around the city and later that night we went to a famous jazz bar. I was usually 95% rap, 5% R&B, but the jazz was a'ight. The conch fritters were good, and Audrey's company was even better. Though I didn't fuck her that night, she promised me all day tomorrow.

Tomorrow did come, most of it spent in a suite at The French Quarters hotel, frolicking in bed, as well in and out of the hot tub.

With Lolita's joke still ringing in my ear, I definitely put on a condom before each of our romps. Audrey kept tryna get me to raw dog the pussy, wanting to feel me bust all up inside of her, but like I said, Lolita's joke had me too shook to roll the dice. If I was gonna die, it would be by the gun—the same way I lived—pussy wasn't takin' me out the game. Fuck dat!

CHAPTER 8

Once we were back in Atlanta, it was quickly back to business. Like all good businessmen, Murder Mike delegated authority so that business operated smoothly and productively even when he was away. The trap and weight money was proper when I picked it up from Corey, the young brave heart from Englewood who'd buried two of Rich Kid's soldiers during the shootout and was elevated to crew chief. The trap money from a spot we had on the Westside was proper also.

I spent half a day with Inez and a few hours with Lil' T. Lonnie went with me by Cheryl's mother's house to check her mail and to search her phone bill and her house for any evidence she'd been in touch with her daughter. She denied hearing anything else from Cheryl, and of course, protested my search of her residence and personal papers. But I wasn't the law and I didn't need a search warrant signed by a judge. She could sit quietly while I took my time searching her shit, or she could get two to the dome.

After finding no evidence of her corresponding with Cheryl, I left her with the warning of what would be her fate if she got cute and put po-po on my ass.

As soon as I dropped Lonnie off, I whipped over to Englewood to get Juanita's address from Miss Pearl. She searched with alcohol-swollen hands until she found Juanita's address in her purse. I copied down the Texas address and left Miss Pearl alone with her best friend, MD 20/20.

Inside of the car, I wrote a short message on the post card: *I enjoyed N'awlins' fine gumbo, jazz and especially the Creole women. But I do remember—You!*

I signed my name, addressed it with no return address, went to buy a postage stamp and dropped the post card in the mailbox by Englewood.

67

Now it was back to business, marking names off the hit list. Our next target was Little Gotti. He'd been laying low since Lonnie and I had fire-bombed his sports bar. He was probably shaking in his shoes, scared to death of the worst enemy a nigga could ever have, the unknown enemy.

Finding Little Gotti was proving harder than we'd anticipated. Partly because he didn't operate drug traps, therefore we couldn't follow the trap money back to him. Little Gotti's MO was dropping weight to several niggaz around the city. Some he dealt with on consignment, others bought keys from him up front.

Murder knew several niggaz Little Gotti dropped weight to, and he contemplated approaching one of them with the ruse that he was looking for a connection, hoping they would then introduce him to Little Gotti. Of course, from there it would've been lights out, but Crazy Nine vetoed that plan.

He told Murder Mike we would work it out when he reached the ATL. "He's on his way here now," explained my mans.

Within hours, the Dread arrived in Atlanta to help us locate our prey.

Crazy Nine greeted me with the same warmth he showed Murder Mike, as if the van incident had never taken place. Maybe Murder Mike had convinced him that I harbored no ill feelings, which wasn't exactly true. I just wasn't in the position to straighten it.

While Crazy Nine was out trying to locate the suddenly invisible Little Gotti, Murder Mike dropped weight around the city and in other spots like La Grange, Moultrie, Columbus and Savannah, Georgia.

I watched his back with a keen eye for the slightest hint of trouble, ready to unleash the AK-47 at the first sign of po-po or a jack move, but nothing foul ever came into play.

Crazy Nine was having no more luck finding Little Gotti than Murder Mike and I had.

Two months later found me and Murder Mike in D.C., the Chocolate City, with plans to leave at least one spot in the city blood red. Jamaican Rick had called us up there to help him remove his primary adversary, a kid from New York known by the name of Born Ruler, who moved down to D.C. and had the dope game on lock.

Jamaican Rick didn't want his workers in Washington, D.C. to do the hit because Born Ruler was well-liked, and Jamaican Rick feared too many niggaz would come gunning for him and his crew if it leaked that they planted Born Ruler in the dirt.

Murder Mike and me would be unknown faces, shifting any heat off of him.

We caught Born Ruler and his two beefy bodyguards at a liquor store where we knew he went to purchase Lotto tickets twice a week. We'd scouted the area for weeks, at night and during the day, planning the best escape route to travel after we did the hit.

I noticed that each time Born Ruler went to the liquor store, he was accompanied by the same two bodyguards. Both were obviously strapped, the unmistakable print of heaters bulging their shirts out at the waist let it be known.

They'd pull the car up to the curb, just a few long strides from the liquor store's front entrance, allowing only seconds when they'd be open for a jack. A pretty decent security plan but with two major flaws.

The first flaw being the assumption that the only harm aimed at Born Ruler would be a robbery attempt. The second and most fatal flaw in their security was their failure to leave someone outside in the car to watch the streets while the others were inside of the store.

I couldn't understand how they could overlook that important aspect of protecting their man. Shit, coming out of the liquor store was when they were most vulnerable. Although one of the body-guards would always exit the store and look around before signaling to Born Ruler that it was safe to come out, it hardly was enough to cause any deviation in our plan.

To anyone entering the liquor store, the two men in gray coverall uniforms and yellow hardhats on the side of the building were two regular city workers, but it wasn't.

It was us and under our hardhats, our hair was covered with do-rags and a stocking cap over that, just to be sure no hair samples would be left inside of the yellow hard hats that we assumed would fall off when we made our getaway.

I had a street sweeper hidden in the weeds between the two buildings where we pretended to be removing bottles and trash. Murder's AK-47 laid beside it, loaded with steel-jacketed hollow points to penetrate bulletproof vests. We each packed a nine inside our coverall pocket in case some fool tried to play Good Samaritan and tackle us after we dropped the heavy artillery and ran.

With gloved hands, we methodically filled bags with empty wine bottles and trash, patiently awaiting the arrival of our target and his henchmen.

They arrived at the curb shortly after 3:00 p.m.

"Remember," I said, already crunk, "you take out the two bodyguards. I'll get Born Ruler, and don't step in front of me! Stay to the side of me or you'll get bodied, too."

Murder said, "Relax, main man. I'm not new to this."

Five minutes later, I saw one of the bodyguards step out on the sidewalk and casually scan the block. He'd seen us two *city workers* on the way into the store, so he paid us no mind.

A fatal mistake.

As soon as the bodyguard nodded to his boss that the block was safe, Murder and I made our move. The shit happened real fast, but it moved in slow motion, damn near freeze framed being in the midst of it.

I heard a bitch's piercing scream immediately after our weapons came into view. Born Ruler took a step backwards, away from the street sweeper and reached for the bulge at his waist, but his reaction was just that, a reaction. I was the quicker one, the offensive one. The street sweeper barked loud and angry. A whole side of Born Ruler's face tore away from his head. The second blast hit him in the chest before his body could hit the sidewalk. Beside me, Murder was earning two more platinum fingernails. His AK-47 fired like when we were kids and we'd light a whole pack of firecrackers at once. Both bodyguards were down and lifeless, but Murder still pumped more steel-jacketed hollow points into them.

"Let's go!" I shouted above the screams and bedlam.

We dipped between the two buildings, hopped over trash bags and dropped the cumbersome weapons in some tall weeds against the side of the liquor store. Taking the exact route we'd charted, we hopped over a chain-link fence and hurried to the bikes that we'd parked on the street that ran behind the two buildings.

Murder Mike had lost his hard hat, mine had stayed on my head, but I tossed it to the ground. The key to the ninja was zipped inside the breast pocket of the coveralls. I quickly retrieved it, unlocked the handlebars and pressed the automatic ignition switch. The bike roared to life. A second later, I heard Murder's bike stall, then it slowly came to life.

I led and he followed, it was important that we traveled a precise, pre-planned route for Jamaican Rick was waiting for us at a certain destination to execute the final leg of our getaway.

Though we'd made several practice rides, in the heat of the moment, it wasn't easy to recognize the proper streets and turns. I almost missed the green house on the corner where I was supposed to turn left. I recognized it at the last second and made the turn, my knee almost scraping the paved street. I checked over my shoulder to make sure Murder was still behind me. He was, but he'd lost control of the bike while executing the last-second turn and went skidding down the middle of the street. The bike slammed into the curb and rolled over onto somebody's front lawn.

I turned around and went back for him. He was injured and limping, but not critically hurt. His bike had fared worse.

"Hop on!" I barked.

A few blocks and turns later, I slowed the bike and rode it up a loading ramp and into the back of a furniture truck. Jamaican Rick didn't ask what had happened to the other bike, he just quickly raised the ramp by pressing the electronic button, closing the truck's rear door, shutting us inside.

Seconds later, I felt the furniture truck pull off.

Murder Mike was a little banged up, with a swollen knee. A little first aid and an Ace bandage had him feeling better, though. I apologized for taking the turn at the last second, forcing him to do the same and lose control of his bike. He brushed off the minor mishap, realizing that the important thing was that we completed the mission we'd traveled to D.C. to handle. We could now return to the ATL under our own power, which beat returning in a box or as headliners in a news article.

We laid low in the chocolate city for a few days, before catching separate flights back to Atlanta.

When I got back to Atlanta, Inez was at home waiting to surprise me. As soon as I walked in the door, I noticed that she was

no longer pregnant. She led me to the bedroom proudly present-
ing our baby girl. Asleep like a tiny angel inside a pink baby crib
with cute pink and white ribbons decorating it.

I picked my daughter up gently, causing her to wail at the top
of her tiny lungs. She'd been born ahead of schedule and was
smaller than any of my other children had been at birth, but she
was completely healthy and as pretty as a lullaby.

Tamia Shanice quieted down when she felt her daddy snuggle
her in the cradle of his arms and rocked her back to sleep.

I then sat down on the edge of the bed, mad experienced with
holding infants, newborns, whatever.

"When did you have her?" I asked Inez, incredulous that already she seemed to have regained her normal figure.

"A week ago yesterday," said Inez. "We tried to wait on you
to get back in town but Tamia was too anxious to come into this
world." She leaned over and kissed our daughter's chubby cheek.

"Oh," she remembered, "I had to give her my last name since
you weren't around to sign the birth certificate, and we aren't
married."

"What?"

"Calm down," laughed Inez, "we can go change her last name
tomorrow."

And we did.

I loved and claimed all mine.

Still crunk from the D.C. episode, I got with Lonnie and we
sat around his crib smoking 'dro and sipping on yak. I got higher
than the Eiffel Tower, so high that I couldn't even recall all the
bodies I had stacked when I tried to add 'em up in my head.

I knew I had more bodies than I had children, and at the rate
I was deading niggaz, it was possible I'd eventually get more
bodies than pussy. I knew that when I hooked up with Murder

Mike tomorrow, he'd have six platinum nails. *He better bless me with some loot!* I was down with the clique but I wasn't murdering niggaz for free.

Him and the Dreads saw their dividends from the sale of dope, mine manifested from my role as enforcer. Bodies paid extra.

High as a mafucka, I started thinking about my two princesses, Eryka and Chanté. Yeah, I still had Lil' T and a new baby girl, but none of a nigga's seeds could take the place of the others. My angels were probably wondering why they didn't see me anymore, too young to verbalize the absence in their lil' hearts. They'd grow up calling a Haitian mafucka Daddy! That was the coldest part of what that bitch Cheryl had done. I didn't wanna think about her fat, lazy ass laying back on some island like she was born rich or like she'd hustled up the loot they were living off of. It probably would've been easier to swallow if she was somewhere, just her and my daughters. But for the bitch to switch wallets with me and run off with a nigga? That shit blew my high.

I thought about my beef with Ma Dukes and that shit vexed me more. I would've given anything for us to have back the relationship we had before she met and married Raymond and got all brand new on me.

Go over there and murk that chump ass nigga and then shit will be back square with you and your moms, the demon inside tried to persuade me.

Luckily for Raymond's ass, I didn't let the demon in me take over. I needed to somehow chill the fuck out before I lost my cool and did some dumb shit.

"Yo, tight man," I said, standing up and giving Lonnie some dap. "I'm about to bounce."

I pulled up to the payphone outside of the Exxon station down the street from Lonnie's crib, grabbed a handful of phone numbers that I kept in my glove compartment and began calling bitches at random. That seemed as good a method as any since I couldn't remember who none of them were anyway.

When they answered their phone, I didn't mince words. I wasn't in the mood to romance anyone, I wanted to fuck something until my anger dissolved.

The first bitch I called hung up on me when I admitted that I couldn't recall how she looked or where we met, but I still wanted to hook up and blow her back out.

I dialed the next number.

"Hello," some nigga answered.

"Yeah, lemme speak to Cookie."

"Who is this?"

"Damn, you nosey, homey."

"Naw, nigga, Cookie is my woman. Where do you know her from?"

"Fool, I been dickin' that bitch for six months," I lied and then hung up on his ass.

Let the trife ho explain that to her jealous nigga.

I didn't get an answer at the next two numbers I called, but persistence paid off. I dialed another number and a sweet, sassy voice answered, "Helloooo!"

"May I speak to Tabitha?" I asked, reading the name written above the number in a pretty little scrawl.

"This is she. Who is this?"

"Youngblood."

"Where I know you from?"

"Fa real, lil' mama, I can't even remember where we met or how you look. I just ran across your number in my glove compartment and right now I'm too high to try to figure all that shit out."

"High?"

"Just weed, shawdy," I chuckled. "I ain't no crackhead. Anyway, I'ma keep it trill. I live a fast and hard life. Every day I wake up it's a blessing. Right now I need to hold something soft to take my mind off of the streets."

"Well, ain't you got a pillow?" Her tone was real sassy but playful.

"Yeah, pillow-soft leather seats in my whip," I replied. "What you know 'bout dat?"

I heard her suck her teeth.

"Check it, lil' mama. I'm talkin' motel, weed, Cristal, sex, the whole nine. If you ain't with it, that's cool. I'll get back at you another day."

"How you gon' invite me to the motel and you don't even know how I look? What if I'm a booger bear?"

"You can't be, 'cause I don't accept shawdies' numbers unless they are tight."

"What type of whip you got?" Tabitha asked.

"I got a money-green Lexus truck and a black Benz drop, both sittin' on chrome," I boasted 'cause I could tell she would be impressed.

"A'ight, you can come pick me up, but if you're ugly, I ain't givin' you no pussy."

That was cool with me 'cause I've been called many names, but *ugly* wasn't one of 'em.

Tabitha gave me directions to her crib out in Forest Park. I already had an ounce of weed, so I only had to stop at the liquor store on the way to Tabitha's crib and copped two bottles of Cristal and a box of Magnums.

Tabitha was waiting at the curb of her driveway when I pulled up in my truck. She looked at me through the rolled-down driver's window, making sure that I wasn't ugly before she ran around to the other side and hopped in.

"What you waitin' on? Let's go!" She hurried me like she was sneaking off. "I remember you now," she said as we drove, but I still couldn't place her face. She looked kinda young.

"How old are you?" I asked.

"You ain't jailbait are you?"

"Tsssk! I'm nineteen, nigga. Are you jailbait?"

I laughed. "Naw, shawdy, I'm just young in the face."

Tabitha wanted to stop at Popeye's before we went to the motel. I wasn't trippin' it. Most shawdies were taught to get somethin' out of a nigga before giving up the pussy. A chicken dinner was a small thing to a giant.

At the motel, we punished our chicken dinners, blew some dro and drank Cristal. Neither of us did much talking. I kept lookin' at Tabitha, tryna figure out where we had met.

"Why you keep starrin' at me?" she asked.

"'Cause you're a cutie." That wasn't a lie. She wasn't dimed up, but she was honey-brown, with deep dimples that enhanced her beautiful smile. Her build was on the slim side but not skinny. She was 'bout a seven maybe an eight.

We were sitting on the bed. I stood up and pulled my Rocawear jersey over my head, tossing it across the back of the chair that was at a table near the bed.

"You ready for some of this?" I popped.

Tabitha tried to act all bashful and shit but ten minutes later, I had her in the buck, long-dickin' the pussy. Of course, I was wrapped up.

The lil' ho's pussy was bigger than a mafucka, sloppy wet but good. I had to play mind games to get her to suck the joystick but then I had to pull her up before she chewed it off!

I hit it again, from the back this time, fell asleep, woke up and smoked a blunt and boned shawdy again.

"Take off the condom," she demanded.

"Nah, lil' mama, I don't roll like that."

"Please. I can't feel you."

"You couldn't feel a truck in yo big ass pussy," I mumbled.

"What you say?" Tabitha looked over her shoulder, ass still in the air.

"Nothin'. Just take this dick," I replied, then I started rough ridin' the pussy.

This time, I blew the bitch's back out.

Around nine-thirty, Tabitha woke me up and said she had to get home. I took a quick shower, dressed, turned in the room key and we bounced.

"Can you stop somewhere and buy me something to eat?" she asked, again putting the charge on me.

I chumped her off with Krystal's and drove her home. She asked me not to pull into her driveway, so I pulled to the curb in front of her house.

As soon as Tabitha's feet hit the pavement, a pretty mocha-complexioned chic stomped out of the house and down the driveway, stopping a foot from my truck, hands on her hips. Much attitude.

"Deidra! Where yo hot ass been?" the mocha-complexioned chic fussed.

"Mama been calling everywhere looking for you. Yo ass in trouble now!" She peeped in my truck. "And who the fuck is you? My sister ain't but fourteen years old!"

Suddenly she recognized my face and I recalled hers. We had met one day I'd taken Lil' T to Chuck E. Cheese. She'd been there with her daughter, who was about my son's age. I remembered her well now. *Her* name was Tabitha. I'd gotten caught up in the streets and forgot all about her.

"Don't I know you from somewhere?" she wondered, still trying to place my face.

"Yeah, we met at Chuck E. Cheese awhile back," I reminded her. "I was there with my son."

"Youngblood?"

"Yep."

"Where do you know my little sister from? With her hot ass!"

"I don't really know her. I was visiting a friend who lives a few blocks from here. I guess his lil' sister and *Deidra* are friends. He asked me to give your sister a ride home since it's dark out."

Deidra clutched her Krystal burgers and smacked her lips. "See, I ain't been doing nothin'!"

I winked at Deidra.

That's right, shawdy. Ain't nothin' wrong with a lie to save your ass. Your secret is safe wit' me.

Once hot ass Deidra disappeared inside the house, the real Tabitha stood at the curb and we talked for a few minutes.

"Why didn't you ever call?" she asked.

"I lost your number."

"It must not have been important to you, then."

"Naw, that's not it," I said. "A nigga just careless with shit like that. Lemme give you my pager number." I wrote it down on a Krystal's napkin and gave it to her. "Get at me."

"I will," she promised, flashing that same cute dimpled smile as Deidra.

I wondered if she had a big ole coochie like her lil' sister.

"Thanks for giving my sister a ride home. She is so damn fast."

Shawdy, you don't know the half, I thought.

CHAPTER 9

The next day, I met with Murder Mike and Crazy Nine at one of the other stash houses in Hapeville, a small city that was really Metro-Atlanta.

As I'd expected, Murder had six platinum fingernails. He obviously hadn't counted Born Ruler on his list of bodies he'd stacked. Though dude's demise was part of a common scheme, I guess he figured it would be frontin' to claim a body he hadn't put a bullet in. I could feel him on that. I wasn't counting the two bodyguards on my mental list, either.

One of the rooms at the stash house was stacked ceiling high with wrapped pounds of hydro weed and ganja, so much weed that I could almost smell it from the street.

Murder told him so, and Crazy Nine sprayed some shit that immediately covered the smell. He gave us props for the D.C. hit, and handed me an envelope full of cash.

For more hours than I care to remember, we compressed pounds of weed and stuffed them up inside of the hollow trunks of cheap ceramic lamps. Then we wrapped the lamps in newspaper and stacked them inside moving boxes, placing a layer of foam between each layer of lamps. We left out five hundred pounds of 'dro and one hundred pounds of ganja to be distributed in Atlanta. The rest, I assumed, were shipped to the other three Dreads.

Money was pouring in from the Englewood traps with the weight being sold. The weed was selling like crazy, but I couldn't tell if Inez' connection was affected by our taking over the bulk of Atlanta's weed business. I'd retired Inez from the game, now that she had my seed, but I wasn't planning on being her cake-daddy, like Fat Stan had been. She already had a job lined up after the baby was three months old.

When I rode through the hood with Murder Mike to check the traps, I'd usually see Cita's Benz parked in front of her mother's unit. I pulled my main man's coat, reminding him that was how the enemy knew where a hustler laid his head, they followed his girl.

"True dat!" he said. And like *poof,* Cita was seldom seen in the hood anymore.

Murder's Ma Dukes and his older brother and sister still lived in the projects, but they didn't know where he and Cita called home. His Ma Dukes was ghetto as hand-me-down clothes. She'd cut a mafucka in a New York minute and her kids could do no wrong in her eyes. I liked her, though.

Murder's older brother, Bobby, was a crackhead, always trying to sell a nigga some meat he'd stolen from a supermarket in the area. Murder's sister was two years older than us. She had two kids by two different niggaz, both of 'em doing time. Her name was Cynthia, but everybody called her Fat Ma.

She'd flirt with me even before I cliqued up in the game with her peeps. I wasn't trying to go there, though, 'cause I damn sho' wasn't gonna wife her. All she could ever be was my bitch on the side and I wasn't gon' fade my main man's sister like that! Besides, Fat Ma was just trying to fuck with a nigga's head. She liked older niggaz who were easier to juice than a thugged-out panty hitter and quitter like me.

I was making loot, enough to floss with and buy the type of shit a young nigga from the hood always dreamed of. But I hadn't come close to getting over the lost mil'. I was so scarred by that shit that I only kept pocket money at Inez' crib. I had my own spot, but I didn't keep my stash there, either. I was seldom at my townhouse, so the neighbors would look at me like I was breaking in when I did go there.

I'd still swing by and holla at Poochie when time allowed. She was still doing good, working, going to church and raising her sons. She told me she was thinking about marrying a preacher man.

I said, "If you do, when they get to the part of the ceremony where they ask if anyone knows a reason why y'all shouldn't be joined together in holy matrimony, I'ma stand up and tell our secrets."

Poochie laughed and then came back with some holy shit. "My God is a forgiving God."

I wanted to say: "Poochie, please! Put down that Bible and let's go fuck up your bed sheets!" But I respected her religious thing. It wasn't like she was trying to convert me or like we couldn't talk without her quoting the scriptures. As long as I wasn't crackin' for some ass, she wouldn't push the Good Book in my face.

She'd tell me how smart Lil' T was and how he had a quick temper like me *and* Shan. Whenever I was with him I talked to him about controlling his temper and always doing his best in school. The shit was somewhat hypocritical 'cause I had never liked school and had a hair-trigger temper, but what was I to do, teach my son to grow up to be a robber and a killer like his pops? Nah, it was my duty as his father to point him down the right road. From there, he could choose to go in any direction he wished. I'd still love him unconditionally, but I would never point him toward wrong.

He was a trip, though, always asking a million questions. I'd bring him over to spend the night at Inez' so he could bond with his baby sister.

Inez' other daughter, Bianca, had begun staying there, too. Now that Inez wasn't selling weed anymore, she wanted Bianca to live with her again. She also wanted Bianca and Tamia to get used to each other. They were sisters after all.

I had no qualms with that. I wasn't a petty nigga. I had nothing against no man's child. I figured, in time, shortie would get used to me being around. It wasn't like I had to baby-sit her.

Lil' T had fun roughing her up, and she got a thrill out of following him around. Tamia, with her precious self, just sucked Inez' nipple and chilled, unless my sister, Toi, came by and spoiled the baby rotten, holding her all day long.

Yeah, Glen was trusting Toi out of his eyesight now that Rich Kid wasn't around. I'd told Toi that one day I was gonna tell Glen I shouldn't have taken our beef so far. Had I known everything that had went down, I probably would've handled it differently. It still didn't justify him fracturing my sister's jaw, but I understood now why he'd snapped. I told Toi that was some trife shit she had done, and not to be putting me in no predicaments like that no more.

She said, "Crazy ass boy! I tried to tell you to let it go."

"Let what go, Daddy?" Lil' T dipped in.

"Let this go." I grabbed him and wrestled him to the floor. Bianca jumped on my back, laughing and squealing, forgetting she didn't like me.

CHAPTER 10

Playtime was over and it was back to business. Little Gotti had resurfaced and word was that he and his blond bombshell got popped in North Cackalackie for trafficking much yayo up the interstate. They'd been in custody without bond the whole time we'd been looking for them.

Now they were free on bond, trying to stack as much loot as possible to make up for their losses in case they had to go do a bid. Other people in the street said they were let out on bond to set niggaz up.

Neither Murder nor I wanted to fuck with Little Gotti, fearing he was under surveillance by the feds. Furthermore, if he'd gotten popped in North Carolina, he'd soon be, doing a bid, eliminating himself from our list.

Murder took our concerns and reasoning to Crazy Nine.

A day later Murder said, "He wants us to stick to the plan," leaving no room for debate.

When Little Gotti and Blondie's execution-style murders were reported in the newspapers a week later, it was confirmed that John "Little Gotti" Bryant had been a recently turned government informant. Police speculated he'd been murdered to keep him from informing on his supplier. They were also investigating to see whether or not there was a leak in their office. Blondie was referred to as his stripper girlfriend, and it was reported that in the case of her murder, the killer had used overkill.

I guess five to the head could be deemed as such.

So my main man got his seventh platinum nail, and I lucked up on sixty grand and two bricks. I joked that Murder was running out of fingers and would have to start on his toes.

I sold the bricks to a nigga Lonnie knew, blessed my tight man for hooking the deal up and took all the cheddar to my new stash spot. Then it was time to unwind.

Although it wasn't quite nine, it was already hot as hell. It was mid-summer, so I wore baggy shorts, a wife-beater, blingin' like The Bird Man with my top down on the whip. I had gotten my hair braided in a fly zigzag pattern by this shawdy in Englewood who usually hooked me up.

I drove the Benz drop to pick up the real Tabitha. She wore loose-fitted Prada shorts and a strapless bikini top, sandals that showed off her pretty feet and a gold ankle bracelet that matched the herringbone around her neck. Long ringlets hung down from under a floppy straw hat.

When she slid into the passenger seat, her sweet fragrance almost put me in a trance. She carried a picnic basket. I took it from her and placed it on the backseat.

We went to White Waters Amusement Park and got on plenty water rides, getting wet and yelling like teenagers. It was good, clean fun.

We chilled later in the picnic area, eating chicken sandwiches, deviled eggs and fresh fruit that Tabitha had put together. Of course, I brought the weed, which we had trouble finding a secluded spot to blow, but we were persistent and it eventually paid off. Before long, we were blazin' 'dro, sitting on a huge rock conversing.

By 4:30, we were on our way back to my crib to change clothes and go see the fireworks show out in Stone Mountain. Knowing our plans, Tabitha had brought a change of clothes with her.

We had a few hours to blow before the fireworks show, so we chilled at my crib, listening to music and gettin' our heads right.

I was so high, I had to let Tabitha drive when it was time to go to Stone Mountain.

Shawdy enjoyed the hell out of the display of fireworks. "Wow! That's sooo pretty," she kept commenting.

Me? I was trippin'. Every time a firecracker popped, I jumped.

Niggaz might be shootin' at me!

I felt naked and paranoid without my heat on my waist. It was a good thing I had left my strap in the car 'cause my paranoia might've caused me to *Blocka! Blocka! Blocka!* the whole goddamn crowd.

"You okay?" Tabitha asked.

"Nah, baby girl, let's bounce."

Back at my crib, I found out that dimples weren't the only thing that ran in the family. Tabitha's pussy was even bigger than Deidra's! A nigga needed twelve inches to hit bottom, and I was short about four.

Since I couldn't hit bottom, I stroked the pussy at an angle, determined to at least beat down the *sides.* Shawdy moaned and scratched big welts on my back.

Hours later, after dropping Tabitha back off at her house, I headed back to mine. *Do You Remember Me* by Jill Scott filled the airwaves.

That's Juanita's song!

I bobbed my head and turned up the volume.

Damn, I miss you girl.

I wasn't tryna feel what I was feelin', so I clicked on the CD player. Jaheim replaced Jill Scott but then that song where Jaheim was singing about a diamond in the rough, a special lady that he let get away, came on and that shit had me missing Jaunita, too.

I hurriedly changed Jaheim to Trick Daddy and rode out.

I told Inez the welts on my back must've come from niggaz fouling me on the basketball court.

"Yeah. Just like two plus two equals ten!" she quipped sarcastically and turned her back to me in bed.

I scooted up close behind her so that my joint was poking her in the butt.

"Oh, it's like that now?" My voice on the back of her neck.

She turned over on her side, facing me, and asked if one woman was ever going to be enough for me.

I was like, "Girl, what are you talkin' 'bout?"

"Play dumb," said Inez. "Yo' ass oughta have enough of fuckin' with trifling hos!"

"What's that supposed to mean?" I frowned, figuring she was referring to Cheryl running off with my loot. If so, it was a low blow. It was unlike Inez to trip like that. *Damn!* Was she about to start serving a nigga baby mama drama, too?

"I take that back. I'm sorry," she said quickly. "I'm just saying, boo. You *could* have the decency to try to hide what you do. If you stop respecting me, what we gon' have then? I ain't tryin' to be your bitch."

"C'mon, shawdy," I hugged her to me. "You know it ain't gon' be like dat. No matter what I do, I come home to you."

"*Hmmpf!* I'm worried about what you gon' bring home to me!" she huffed.

I reached down and picked up my jeans off of the floor, the ones I'd just taken off. I pulled out a roll of condoms and flashed them in her face.

"I ain't raw dogging with nobody but my boo," I said, hugging and kissing her all over the face.

"Still," Inez said, fighting off my kisses, "I'll be glad when you outgrow your ho-hoppin'."

88

"I'ma chill, shawdy," I promised, knowing I was lying as the words left my mouth.

Ca$h

CHAPTER 11

A major drug war jumped off in the city, but me, Murder Mike, and 'em weren't involved. The beef was allegedly between BCF, José and the Ese's.

Two members of BCF got slayed outside of their recording studio in Buckhead. In retaliation, five ese's were found murked in an apartment out in Gwinnett. It didn't cost us anything to lay back and wait for the gun smoke to clear and then go after whichever crew was left standing.

We were recruiting young soldiers and killers who we could use to build strong traps in many of the known drug neighborhoods. Young niggaz who'd slang rocks all day and night, as well as light a spark in a nigga's dome if they opposed 'em or tried to take what they were out to earn.

We had to go to St. Louis once, Murder and me, to dome a coupla neighborhood superstars who fought Rohan a little too hard to keep their titles as the city's major coke suppliers. In the end, I put half a clip in one of 'em just for being stubborn, while Murder Mike's eighth platinum nail said all that needed to be said about the other major supplier who'd fought hard, but in vain.

While things were at a peaceful existence, I got with Lonnie and we bullshitted a day away. We got blazed and talked about stupid ass Blue, who'd been found guilty of robbing and murdering the Rib's Lady and her daughter. The Rib Lady's grown children had pushed for the death penalty and got it. Now junkie ass Blue was on his way to death row, courtesy of his jones for crack.

Since I was no longer a robber, per se, Lonnie had started back to taking Shotgun Pete on licks with him again. I wasn't mad at him about it. In fact, I understood his reasoning. A nigga's life be on the line every time he puts on that ski mask. He had to have somebody with him he knew wouldn't panic and leave him with no backup if shit got do-or-die.

I couldn't be mad. Shit, Pete hadn't done a thing to Lonnie. His violation was against *me*. Lonnie still had to get money. I was gettin' mine, doing my thing.

Murder Mike was my partner and *he* didn't like Lonnie. Well, he didn't trust him. Which was one and the same in my head 'cause how you gon' like a nigga you can't trust? And vice-versa. So I guessed if I could roll with Murder Mike and not be violating my friendship with Lonnie, he could roll with Shotgun Pete and not be violating me.

Whatever.

Lonnie spanked me all day at video games 'cause I hadn't played in a while, too busy defeating much more dangerous foes at games that were true life or death.

However, these days business was operating relatively smooth. My heater was getting a chance to go cold, and my primary job was watching Murder Mike's back and picking up loot from different spots. I was trusted to be around the stash houses when the money from all the traps were being counted or when a load of dope arrived to be cooked into crack and dispensed to our dealers and workers, and especially when all four Dreads came to Atlanta once a month to meet with my main man and discuss the state of their respective affairs.

I'd even gone along with Murder Mike when the monthly meeting was held in D.C., St. Louis or Cali. I was being groomed to hold down a whole city, in case we eventually expanded our operation or if tragedy should claim one of those already in that position.

Still, I felt I lacked a few of the natural instincts in that area that true dope boys, like Murder and 'em, possessed to the max. I never got hyped about a new shipment of dope like Murder would. I didn't like anything but one aspect of the dope game—the Benjamin's. The rest was too much fuckin' work and there wasn't no end in sight.

Where was the finish line? After we erased those from our hit list, could we consider the game over and won? Not hardly. We'd have to be even more ruthless to remain on top.

The way I figured it, there was always gonna be some mayhem on the horizon with us pushing yayo. Niggaz wouldn't let us live in peace. Somebody gon' want what we got bad enough to come after it. Plus, when your shine glows the brightest, who the Feds gon' aim at?

From what I sensed, Murder Mike thought the dope game was like a job with the state, lifelong. Or like a couple's wedding vows, 'til death do us part, unless it parted in a costly, messy divorce, but never without great loss and pain. I guess true dope boys couldn't see that. They were like a love-sick nigga who couldn't let go of a no-good, trife-ass bitch. Me? I wasn't love-sick over no bitch or the game. So my commitment wasn't infinite.

But I kept that to myself.

Ca$h

CHAPTER 12

José caught it leaving the ESPN Zone sports bar on Peachtree. The streets said that a coupla BCF niggaz Swiss-cheesed him and four other ese's. I was reading about it in *The Atlanta Journal/Constitution* while chillin' with Inez, her daughter, Bianca, Lil' T, and Tamia, who was growing as fast as a chicken on steroids.

Inez was asking me if I would mind if she sent Bianca's father, Fat Stan, some money for commissary.

"His mother called over here saying he needs some money and she's on a fixed income and ain't got…"

I looked up from the paper, "You can send him *your* money," I said and then made myself clear. "Out of the check you get from work, but you bet' not send that nigga one penny of nothing with *my* blood and sweat on it!"

The reason I didn't trip over Inez sending Fat Stan some loot was because, number one, if it was in her heart to send it, she'd find a way to do it without my knowing. Number two, she did show respect by asking if I'd mind. And, last but not least, to *not* allow her to send the fat nigga a lil' help would've been training Inez to allow another nigga to stop her from throwing *me* a rope if I ever needed her help and we weren't together anymore. A nigga had to think ahead, even if the way he was living doesn't promise tomorrow.

My pager started beeping.

I saw Murder Mike's cell phone number flash across the tiny screen. I would've normally gone to a payphone to call Murder back, but Tamia was running a summer fever and would cry her lungs out when I tried to lift her up from my lap.

"Lemme use your cell phone," I told Inez.

She handed it to me. I flipped it open and dialed Murder's number.

"Main man, whud up?" I asked as soon as he answered.

"Turn on the news!" he said excitedly.

I quickly grabbed the remote off of the coffee table in front of me and aimed it at the flat screen TV against the wall. Inez sat down beside me on the sofa and watched as a serious-faced reporter spoke live from outside of Street Life Productions recording studio.

"Just about an hour ago, federal agents, along with ATF agents, raided this studio and arrested five men believed to be members of the Black Crime Family, an alleged drug gang with ties to the music industry," the man reported.

He went on to report that, *"In coordinated raids at two other allegedly-owned BCF businesses, more than two dozen arrests were made, including the arrest of Antonio 'Baby Boy' Williams, the reputed crime boss of the family,"* the reporter concluded as the picture of Baby Boy appeared on the screen.

"Back to you, Monica."

"Thank you, Dan," replied the anchor woman. *"Police say that the BCF is responsible for the gang-style murders outside the ESPN Zone last week. They believe…"*

I clicked off the television, putting an end to the report.

"Damn!" I exclaimed to Murder Mike.

"I'ma holla back, whoady. Lemme call Crazy Nine."

With José slumped and the BCF cased-up, we were now the strongest crew standing, and we'd already prepared for the day.

Niggaz now said the Dreads ran the city, acknowledging that Murder Mike was the Dreads number one-point man. I was viewed as a lieutenant and right-hand man. The streets bowed down to our power. I could see it in mafuckaz eyes, everywhere we went. I was seeing so much money pass through the stash houses, I saw dead presidents in my sleep.

There were other, less powerful crews operating around the city. Some dudes pushing weight, but they were no real threat to our throne. Either they were clocking what we now considered minor figures, or their dope came from us directly or indirectly.

It was impossible for any one crew to supply all the dope to a certain city, especially one as large and welcoming as the ATL. So unless a crew began to hurt our pockets, we didn't sweat 'em. Besides, I agreed with Crazy Nine when he explained to Murder Mike that if we were to become the *only* supplier in the city, we'd also be the only mafuckaz who could get busted. Our plan was to remain the major supplier, the main dog in the drug flow.

The longer the Big Dogs in the BCF remained locked up awaiting trial on federal racketeering charges, the more arrests were being made throughout the city. Niggaz were turning on their own blood, tryna get the best plea deal possible.

Me and Murder Mike bounced to N'awlins in case the Feds' dragnet in ATL had us in their sights. Crazy Nine wanted us to remain there until the city cooled off.

Inez understood the game, trusted a nigga's heart and asked no questions. *"Just call me when you can,"* was her only request.

On the other hand, Cita wanted to come with Murder Mike. *"Why can't you take me with you?"* she cried. *"What you got to hide?"*

"Look, girl!" he said, frustrated with her drama. *"Being with me ain't too safe right now."*

"So!" she protested.

"You ain't goin' and that's all to it. Now, you can either chill the fuck out or get your eye blacked!"

Of course Cita chose the black eye.

In N'awlins, as soon as our whips pulled into Francisca's driveway and Murder Mike saw her and the twins, Michael and Michelle, he transformed from Nino Brown to Cliff Huxtable. I kidded him about it when Fran wasn't around, but I made the same transformation when I was with my shorties.

Fran was such a contrast to Cita. My nigga had to have had split personalities to deal with both of them. Fran was definitely worthy of the wifey title bestowed upon her. As for Cita, I understood why my dawg fucked with her, but he put up with more of that bitch's theatrics than I would have. She was a nigga's downfall waiting to happen.

Even though Fran seemed perfect, I wondered if she had a nigga on the side to keep her company when Murder was in the ATL.

Again, Lolita was the first to get the dick when I got to N'awlins. The next day, I hit Audrey off with a little sex, but I backed up from shawdy when she said, *"Don't make me put roots on you, nigga, to keep this dick all to myself."*

"Roots? Girl, that shit don't work."

"Yes, it does. My girl put roots on her baby daddy. Now his dick can't get hard with no other bitch but her," Audrey swore, laughing.

I laughed right along with her, but the more I thought about it, the more afraid I was to kick it with Audrey, so I began ducking the bitch like she was my PO.

It was still on and poppin' in N'awlins, especially since it was around the time for the Bayou Classic. Grambling University and Southern University were meeting in their annual football game, and the city was swamped with shawdies. The drop top Benz attracted the hos and my swagger reeled 'em in.

When I wasn't running up in one chick or another, I was chillin' in my hotel room, blowing purp' and listening to CDs.

Tupac would have me wanting to murder something or wanting to hunt down Cheryl and her Haitian nigga, and do 'em both.

I'd think about my two lil' princesses, Eryka and Chanté, trying to recall every little detail about them. Savoring the memories, as my heart ached for them, I felt tears sliding down my face. *I miss y'all so much.*

The pain almost made a young G sob fo' real. I thought about calling Inez, shawdy would've understood. I didn't make the call, though. I didn't want her to hear the tears in my voice. Instead, I called Toi, and we talked well into the night.

Finally, I said, "I'll call you when I touch back down in the city. I'm 'bout to lay it down and get some sleep."

"Okay. Bye. I love you."

"Love you, too. And thanks, sis."

"Boy, you ain't gotta thank me. I'm family. Anyway, you need to stop tryna act like don't nothin' bother you. Everybody got feelings," said Toi.

When we returned to ATL, the city was dryer than a desert. It was just as hard for a smoker to find a rock as it was to hit the Lotto. A nigga had to smoke homegrown if he wanted some weed. The feds had snatched up most of the city's major playaz.

Only a month had passed since BCF got snatched up. Their fall, other subsequent arrests, and *our* little hiatus had crippled the city's drug flow, but not for much longer. Crazy Nine arrived in town with a trailer of werk, and we put our hustle down strong. Me totin' that steel and watching Murder's back every step of the way.

When winter turned into spring, I moved into a big five-bedroom house with three bathrooms, a den, a large eat-in kitchen, a patio and a pool in back. It was out in the 'burbs and would've cost three hundred grand had I bought it. But I was thinking that whenever I walked away from the game, I was walking far away, so why waste loot on buying the crib?

Now I was living in the suburbs, a necessary precaution to keep potential enemies from locating me too easily. Inez still kept her crib but she was with me more than not. Her presence wasn't stopping me from hittin' other pussy 'cause I was never about taking hos to where I laid my head anyway. As long as they had motels, hotels and backseats in whips, I was never short of a place to bone a ho.

Speaking of hos, they had already been choosing a young nigga. Now they acted like groupies when I showed my mug on the scene, and not just the bitches in the hood, the professional bitches were all on a young nigga's dick the few times I hung in their circles. Those hos were as phony as the rocks crackheads be selling to stupid white boys that come to the hood and give their money to the first mafucka they see posted on the curb.

I understood why Murder Mike wanted to fuck with females that had more class than Cita, but I'ma just be real about it. Give me a shawdy from the hood any day over those fake hos who grew up in neighborhoods where every house had a daddy in it. Just as long as my hood shawdy ain't alley and dumb.

Still, I boned a few flight attendants, a paralegal and too many bitches with their own businesses to remember. When a nigga had loot, he was radiant and hos of *all* backgrounds could spot it.

I was convinced that females were born with a sixth sense, the ability to spot a nigga with loot. Hos that I had absolutely nothing in common with were willing to overlook that small incompatibility since I pushed a Benz drop and had laced pockets.

I had sold my Lexus truck and copped a brand new Cadillac Escalade, pearl white exterior, 26-inch rims, pearl white and black swirl leather interior, suede visors, door panels and headrests with Panasonic flat screens and DVD player. I also expanded my wardrobe, but it was all urban gear.

I had hooked up with Tabitha a coupla more times, but that shit fizzled quickly 'cause I wasn't feelin' no chick but Inez. Murder Mike was now pushin' a black Ferrari. His wardrobe was versatile and ran extensive from faded baggy jeans to custom tailored Armani, depending on the occasion.

For the past five or six years mad mafuckaz in the rap and music industry at-large had been migrating to the Dirty South. Now Atlanta was home to mad superstars in that industry. Plus, the ATL had its home-bred superstars, like Jermaine Dupri, Outkast, Goodie Mob, T.I., Toni Braxton, Monica and a slew of others. We'd bump into them all at certain clubs or restaurants. Mad video hos would be at the hot spots, all on major players' dicks.

I wasn't sitting on a mil', but my shine was still bright. My rep attracted those type of hos, too. Most bitches were mad attracted to a nigga with enough power to rule the streets because they knew he had to be way above the average dude. They were curious to share that thug passion with a nigga who was rumored to rule over other thug niggaz and murk his enemies.

Although we occasionally partied and enjoyed our spot on top of the game, neither myself nor Murder Mike made club-going a habit or routine. We understood how disastrous that could be. Besides, Rich Kid was still alive, and there was no telling when he'd resurface and strike back.

Ca$h

CHAPTER 13

Summer came around after months of no major drama in the game, or in a nigga's life.

I'd been in St. Louis for the past week, where I met with all four Dreads and discussed business while Murder Mike was on vacation in N'awlins.

The Midwest was cool, but I was glad to get back home. With Murder on vacation, it fell to me to handle his duties while he was away. I hated fuckin' with dope, even when I was giving it to the niggaz who dispersed it out to our traps and our other workers. It was just too easy to get setup.

Kyree was home from prison. We had hooked up a few times and I broke him off some cheddar so he wouldn't be forced to try a stunt on nobody. We were still a'ight even though I hadn't remained in touch with him and his sister, Brenda, had told him an exaggerated version of what went down between us. My nigga wasn't beefin' about that, it had been too long ago. Plus, he respected a nigga's realness. Kyree knew I was gangsta and couldn't be checked without bloodshed.

"Nigga, you look like Shaft!" Murder Mike cracked on my super-fro as I got out of my whip, having just pulled up in the shoe in Englewood to meet him.

Keisha put in her two-cents. "You do look like you out of the nineteen-seventies. I ain't never seen you with your hair picked out."

"I ain't never seen you with yo' mouth closed," I shot back, snidely. "Y'all just don't know style," I said. Me and Murder dapped hands.

"Whud up, fool?" he greeted me.

"Same story, different day. Whud up?"

Wasn't no business on his mind. He'd just wanted to meet in Englewood and show our presence, a reminder to our soldiers down in the trenches that we weren't too good to visit the hood. Also, our visit reminded them and the brave heart, who was the Englewood crew chief, that we'd check on them unannounced to make sure they were on the grind and not bullshittin'.

The hood remained the same no matter the season. No new faces, just a year older. Blue and a handful of other faces were absent from the horseshoe, having blew trial and gotten trapped in the unforgiving jaws of southern justice with its equally unforgiving penal system.

Keisha was now pushin' some werk, coming up a little nicely. I guess she had a front row seat for so long she had watched and learned how to roll. Whenever I came across some weight, I would hit her with it. Shawdy was proving to be about her business.

Angel came over to where we stood, looking straight dyke with a short Caesar haircut, baggy jeans and a Falcons jersey. She resembled nothing of the cutie I'd freaked at the hotel with Keisha a year and some months ago. I was almost regretting that I had introduced her and Keisha to that girl-girl sex 'cause now Angel looked like a handsome nigga instead of the cute shawdy she'd been before that night.

"Hey, y'all," she spoke to me and Murder.

My main man nodded.

I said, "Whud up, ma? Or is it Papi now?" Smirking as I waited for Angel's response.

"It's still ma, nigga!" she responded defensively. "You ought to know that. Or have you forgotten what's under these clothes?"

"I know what *was* under 'em last year, but shit obviously done changed," I said. "Whatever you do, though, is a'ight with me." 'Cause it really was. I lived and let live. But I couldn't help thinking about how turned on Angel had been that night at the hotel when I coerced her and Keisha into a ménage trio with me. Obviously Angel's first taste of pussy had turned her the fuck out.

"Anyway," Angel said. "Y'all heard about Miss Pearl?"

Changing the conversation. "Naw. What about her?" I queried.

"Oh," said Keisha, "she died from a stroke, a few days ago."

Murder lost interest in the conversation, death not connected to the game and not earning him another platinum nail was not worthy of his time. But Miss Pearl's death was of great interest to me because I knew Juanita would be affected and may need a shoulder to cry on. I was thugged-out, but I always had concern for those who had genuine concern for me.

I asked Keisha and her boyfriend, Angel, if they had seen Juanita. Angel told me that Juanita had been in Englewood the other day, cleaning out her mother's apartment and collecting Miss Pearl's personal things. I told her to find out when and where Miss Pearl's funeral would be and to call my cell and let me know.

"Don't forget," I reminded them. "And I'ma have some more werk for you soon, Keisha."

A nigga like me didn't do funerals unless it was fam or *me* in that box. Usually, if I went inside of a church, there was a safe up in there that I was after, or a mafucka I had to murk, but couldn't corner anyplace else, was in attendance.

So I waited outside of the church until the service was over, and the mourners drove in a slow caravan to the cemetery where Miss Pearl would be laid to rest. I followed at the rear of the procession and then waited in my drop while the mourners went to the grave site saying their final goodbyes before the casket was lowered into the ground.

Juanita was dressed solemnly in a simple black dress and looked as distraught as someone who'd just lost her Ma Dukes would be expected to look. She returned to the funeral home's limo, walking wearily at the elbow of a dude dressed in an army uniform.

Her brother, I figured.

Although I hadn't seen him in years and wasn't positive it was him. I was glad she spotted me as I walked up to intercept her because I really didn't know what I would say to get Juanita's attention. *"Sup, shawdy?"* would've been out of place.

"Hi," I managed to say. "I'm real sorry to hear about your mother."

"Thank you." She broke out in a loud sob.

I wrapped my arms around her. "I'm here for you."

"I really need it right now," she admitted.

"C'mon, let me take you home with me so you can relax. Is that okay with you?"

"Yes."

I gently took her hand and led her to my car.

Later that evening, we sat inside my living room. Juanita was understandably solemn and quiet. I had no words to lessen her loss, so I just held her in my arms in a consoling embrace, not at all sexual.

She fell asleep in my arms, bone weary from grief and travel. I just sat there and held her until she woke up after an hour of rest. Juanita was staying at my house that night. I planned to take her to the airport to catch her flight back to Las Vegas in the morning.

"I just moved out there two weeks ago," she said, her grief-stricken voice almost a whisper. "I had sent Mama my new address and told her to give it to you if she saw you." Her eyes

106

teared at the mention of her Ma Duke. "Oh," she continued after regaining her composure, "thanks for the postcard. How was New Orleans?"

"It's decent down there," I said, recalling my visit to N'awlins over a year ago.

I convinced Juanita to let me take her to Justin's to put a meal in her stomach and take her mind off of grieving for at least a short time.

She dressed simple for dinner but still was every inch as beautiful as I recalled her being the day she'd driven away. She had a combination of strength and determination mixed with a fragility that made her more appealing than any female I knew.

Despite the sudden death of her mother, Juanita was at peace with her new life. She hadn't been in Nevada long enough to tell me much about it, other than that it was hot and had a lot of flat land and few trees.

I admired the courage it must have taken to move so far away from everyone she knew, so she could pursue her academic dreams.

"I see the streets are being good to you." she said and then added, "For now." Obviously referring to the crib.

"I'm only leasing the house. I don't own it."

"I hope you get out of the game before it turns on you, whether you ever come back to me or not," she said.

"I'll do my best not to let the game win," I promised.

"Please do."

We talked for another hour, or so, and then we decided to get some sleep.

That night we slept in bed together but didn't do anything more than sleep.

Morning came too fast for my taste. I had enjoyed holding Juanita all night. And almost before I knew it, we had eaten breakfast and was on our way out of the door.

"I wish you didn't have to leave," I said as I drove her to catch her flight.

"I wish you could come with me." She looked over at me, hopefully.

I knew that wish couldn't come true, not now. And since there was no way to lessen either of our disappointment, I didn't respond.

At the airport, I gave Juanita a gift bag from Chanel.

"You'll come to me one day, I honestly believe that," Juanita said as she wiped at her tears.

I didn't comment. *What could I say?* I just kissed her tears and told her not to let any of those college boys steal her heart.

When she left to board the flight back to Nevada and a life so much different from mine, I felt an emotion I thought no longer existed in me.

Whenever Juanita looked inside the Chanel bag, she would find five thousand dollars, the repayment of the loot she'd given me, and she would find a diamond-encrusted breast pin of two inter-locking hearts. Along with a note that read: *I don't know how to say it, so I gave you this gift to speak for me. Signed, Youngblood.*

Also inside the bag was a CD by the artist Musiq Soulchild, the single *Love.*

I walked out of the airport terminal, hopped in my Escalade, put in a rap CD and hit flip-mode, pushing the vibe I'd just felt for Juanita into the cellars of my mind.

Last night had reminded me how much I dug Juanita. We'd slept peacefully, hugged up, despite the tragedy she was grieving and the fast pace of my life. Even without having sex, I'd enjoyed being with her and waking up with her in my arms.

Besides Inez, who was damn near like a niggaz' comfort and convenience, I had never slept in bed with a woman with no plans of dicking 'em until that night. Juanita held that distinction alone.

Snoop Dogg bumped out the system as I whipped the Escalade. His lyrics helped remind me that *no* female was special, barely.

Ca$h

CHAPTER 14

Another year passed so fast it seemed like somebody had hit the fast-forward button on a nigga's life. No one had challenged our stronghold on the dope game in Atlanta, but we hadn't gained control of any politicians or police officials like Crazy Nine said we'd need in order to have a long reign on the throne. We hadn't accomplished our objectives in the other states yet, either.

We'd made significant progress, but it was proving much harder to gain control of St. Louis, D.C. and especially southern Cali than we'd anticipated.

I'd bodied another nigga in D.C. and Murder Mike had flown out to Cali and returned with two more platinum fingernails on his hand. He'd have to use toenails if he stayed in the game and continued murking niggaz, which was real likely. As for me, I still wasn't rich, but I was living good and stackin' paper.

These days, Lonnie remained my tightman, the one nigga I would trust over all others in my life, including fam. It surprised me that Pete and I had squashed our beef and, though we didn't hang out together, we sometimes wound up at Lonnie's crib at the same time.

Kyree had tried the nine-to-five thing, punching a time clock, but it was too slow delivering the type of things he wanted. Now he sold weed and went on licks with Lonnie and Pete.

Toi was still with Glen, and still lovesick. I wasn't trippin'. He knew not to ever hurt my peeps again. I'd talked to him on the phone several months ago, and we had made peace. But in my mind, we could never be friends. I had busted caps in him. Even if he claimed to forgive it, I would never trust him.

Speaking of forgiveness, I still had none for Ann, the woman who birthed me. Toi was constantly trying to get me to call Mama or to go by there with her. She'd given Mama my new pager number, and Mama had paged me twice. I called her back. I didn't hate her, but our conversations never lasted longer than a few minutes, as she and I still blamed the other one for our not speaking.

I let Toi take Lil' T and Tamia by to see Mama. Inez had gone with her so that she could meet Mama, too. Afterwards she remained in touch with my mother and would take Tamia to see her sometimes, but she knew better not to try to play peacemaker.

Lil' Terrence was every bit of me, just not as adverse to school as I'd been at his age, but physically he was all me. Tamia, who on the other hand, looked more like her mother, Inez. Though she also resembled baby pictures I remembered seeing of Toi, my lil' girl was already walking and getting into everything, just like Eryka.

I still hadn't found a trace of Cheryl or my daughters. Though I continued to make periodic searches of her mother's home, I hadn't found one slip of paper that indicated Cheryl had contacted her mother.

Some college graduate, a highly intelligent fool, had hired Inez to work at a bank. She'd been employed there for eight months now, enjoying honest work more than she'd expected to. I told her if she ever saw a foolproof way I could come in and cleanout the vault, to let me know.

"They have security out the ass," she said. But I had no doubt that Inez would do some Bonnie and Clyde shit with me if times ever got that drastic. I guessed whoever hired her didn't know that.

As loyal as we were to one another, in a way, I was getting bored with Inez. She was still mad crazy 'bout a nigga, and she was even finer since having my daughter, but our relationship was growing stale. I hadn't started neglecting her, yet, but I was definitely looking for another shawdy. Not that I would've replaced Inez with her. I'd never dis shawdy like that. She'd shown mad loyalty and I'd do the same. But I'd spend a lot of nights with a new shawdy if I could find one real enough to warrant it.

I knew where *one* well worth my time resided, but I wasn't trying to pack up and jet to Nevada.

Occasionally, I'd get with Keisha and blow her back out. She was still bumpin' pussies with Angel, but she was too sprung on this thug passion to go strictly veggie. Plus, I was frontin' her four bricks at a time, and shawdy was coming up good in the hood.

One day, I was in the projects freestyle battle-rapping against a cat from up North named Swag who had moved to the Dirty with his cousins in Englewood. We were going back and forth, cuttin' each other down with lyrical venom. A huge crowd had gathered around. Not too many niggaz knew that I rapped, so I surprised them with my flow. But dude was nice with his shit, so I couldn't just chew him up.

A dude named Sheep was supplying the beats by drumming on the hood of an abandoned car. Wanting to end the battle once and for all, I spat:

I was raised on collard greens and cornbread/ I'm that Dirty South nigga/ You keep talkin' out ya head/ I'll be that go in ya mouth nigga/ Throw that 'bo in ya mouth nigga/ That fo-fo in ya mouth nigga/ When my chrome split ya dome/ No more runnin' ya mouth nigga/ When that Brougham takes you home/ I'm still runnin' the South nigga/ The streets respect my name/ 'Cause murda murda is my game/ Yo, why waste my time with this lame?/ I clap niggaz fo' the dough, shawdy/ You rap niggaz just want the fame/ Y'all tell this up-North pussy what's my name.

"Youngblood!" Keisha shouted on cue, and I rapped on.

Yeah, that's who the fuck I be/ A trill nigga who gets paid for that murda shit/ But Up-North niggaz I clap 'em for free/ Take that to ya head like stale cornbread/ Keep slippin' on Dirty South niggaz/ We gon' send you home dead!

The crowd went ape! Swag, the up-North cat, couldn't do shit but bow down.

"Sun, you wicked," he paid props and gave me dap.

"You real nice yourself," I acknowledged. "But this my hood. You can't win down here."

"Sho' can't!" Keisha chimed in.

"Bitch, shut da fuck up!" yelled a nigga named Zay, who used to slang for Rich Kid.

"Yo, nigga, who you callin' a bitch?" I asked, steppin' up in his grill. My hand was at my waist, grippin' heat.

"Naw, Youngblood, I was talking to Keisha, not you," he explained, about to piss on himself.

"Nigga, I know damn well you wasn't talkin' to me, but Keisha is *my* bitch, so apologize to her."

I pulled out my heat. I could tell Zay didn't wanna be punked in front of the whole hood, but the nigga knew that I was *trained to go*, so he didn't test my G.

"I'm sorry, Keisha, my bad," he uttered.

"A'ight, kick rocks, nigga!" I barked. "You ain't from Englewood, no way."

Zay, who was really from Scottsdale, walked off like the lame he was.

CHAPTER 15

One day my pager started beeping, back to back to back. I was at Lonnie's crib getting blazed with him, Delina, Pete and Kyree. I saw that it was my mother's phone number flashing across the screen. No need to go to a pay phone to call her back, she wouldn't want to discuss anything illegal, so it was cool to dial her from Lonnie's home phone.

"Yeah?"

"Have you heard from Toi lately?" my mother asked.

"Not since early last week."

"Well, I'm worried about her," said Ann, her voice reflecting her words. "I've been trying to reach her all week. I even went by her house yesterday and no one answered the door."

I told her Toi had probably gone out of town with Glen.

"No. She would've called to let me know. She was supposed to pick up a prescription for me. I've been sick. If she'd gone out of town, I'm sure she would've let me know to pick up the medicine myself."

I didn't know if my mother knew Toi's boyfriend was a hustler, but I knew he was. Therefore, there were many reasons why him and my sister might go out of town without telling anyone, first. Maybe they'd gone to pick up drugs from Glen's supplier.

"Toi probably forgot about your prescriptions, Ma," I said, not wanting to mention Toi boyfriend's business.

I didn't begin to share my mother's worry until another week passed without either of us hearing from Toi. I went by Toi's crib. Her and Glen's whips were in the parking lot, but no one answered the door. My mother filed a Missing Person report with the police.

A couple days later, the police searched my sister's apartment. Though Mama told me they found no evidence of a disturbance inside of the apartment, they suspected foul play because they'd found Glen's keys still in the ignition, and Toi's purse inside of the truck on the floorboard.

My mother was hysterical. I was extremely worried, but I tried to convince myself that Toi would show up any day with a logical explanation.

A few days later, my mother's worst fear was confirmed. Police notified her that both Toi and Glen's bodies had been found. The brief news article that appeared in the paper the following day said that a jogger had discovered the two decomposed bodies along a seldom used path where he sometimes went to exercise and run.

The wooded area was less than two miles from Toi's apartment. An autopsy revealed that Toi and Glen and had both been shot, point-blank twice, in the back of the head. The police had no suspects. I had a prime suspect in mind, unless Glen had crossed someone in his drug dealings, someone I didn't know.

The days leading up to my sister's funeral, and even the funeral itself, still remained somewhat hazy in my mind. For one, Toi's murder fucked me up so bad I started snorting cocain. I snorted so much coke it was amazing I didn't OD.

I was in such rage and grief I wanted to kill the whole world! I knew what Glen's line of work had been, knew that any number of things could've led to his murder and Toi could've just been unfortunate to be with him when his enemies struck.

The police had found money and drugs inside of Toi's apartment and inside of her purse, which was found in Glen's truck as well as money inside of Glen's pocket.

Robbery wasn't a motive, which meant their murders had been a hit.

Rich Kid!

But why would Rich Kid have Glen murdered, too? On the other hand, if Glen was the intended target, why did Toi get murked? Of course no one knew the answers to those questions better than me. An experienced hitman left no witnesses if he could help it. Instinct screamed Rich Kid, but I'd never known him to send a message to his enemy by having someone close to them killed. He'd just have the enemy murked and be done with it. However, he would definitely know that Toi's death would hurt me deeper than anything.

At the funeral, my mother sat in the front row, a few seats over from me. Her husband, the man who'd really caused our fallout, sat by her side trying to comfort her. But his hand on top of hers had little power over the extreme grief that was painfully evident in her loud sobs. It hurt me deep to see her so torn up, which was how I knew that I still loved the woman who gave birth to me. Our estrangement had been all about anger. My sister's death had brought us two seats from one another, dealing with our loss in two different ways.

While my mother was visibly hurting, I was stoic, with no tears. No one loved that girl inside of the closed soft-pink casket more than I did. No one was hurting inside more than me. Not only had I lost a sister, Toi had been my best friend, my confidant. I was convinced it was my actions that led to her death.

The church was crowded with Toi's friends from the hood, friends she'd met through Glen, friends of Mama's and people who were there as a gesture to me: Lonnie, Kyree, Shan, Pete and many others. Of course Inez was there, too, but not Murder Mike. He didn't do funerals.

"No disrespect," Murder explained, *"but funerals produced bad karma."*

I could understand his position. If it hadn't been family, I would've felt the same. I got up and walked out of the church five minutes after some preacher, who hadn't seen Toi since she was a little girl, started reading passages out of the Bible, trying to relate them to my sister. The shit he was saying had nothing to do with Toi! That holy mafucka hadn't known my peeps! I walked out before I was tempted to pull the heater from my waist and send *him* to a better place. I couldn't even go to the cemetery and listen to more of his bullshit.

Months after Toi was buried, I still had no clear answer as to who was responsible for murdering her. Like me, Murder Mike suspected Rich Kid, but we'd seen no sign of him back in Atlanta. All we could find out was that he checked out of the hospital in Maryland, which meant he *could've* been responsible for my sister's murder.

All doubts were removed and my suspicions confirmed when I got a page one day. I stopped at a payphone and called the number showing on the screen.

"Hello? Who paged Youngblood?" I asked when the phone was answered.

"Bitch nigga, you missed! But I didn't!"

All I heard next was the dial tone.

Rich Kid! I knew that voice without a doubt.

I dialed the number again, hoping he'd answer. I was going to invite his punk ass to some real cowboy shit. Me and him, face to face, guns blazin'! But his punk ass never answered. Eventually, a chick answered the phone and told me it was a payphone near Georgia Baptist Hospital.

Crazy Nine gave me two weeks to settle the score with Rich Kid. Then he expected me to put business over personal matters.

I understood that the show still had to go on but my heart wasn't in it.

I did what my role on the team required, but with even less passion for the game than I'd had before Toi was killed.

Females were even no distraction from what I was feeling. I wasn't in the mood for their stupid asses. Inez tried her best to help stem my anger but it was too great.

Late one Saturday evening, I headed out the door of Inez' crib.

"I'm going to my sister's grave."

"Let us go with you," said Inez, holding Tamia on her hip. Bianca had gone to visit her father in prison with Fat Stan's mother.

"Nah, shawdy, I'm good," I told Inez. She could sense my head wasn't right.

"Please, baby," she pleaded, looking at the bottle of Henny in my hand and the burner on my waistband. I guess she was concerned about my state of mind.

"I wanna go alone," I replied, giving her and Tamia a good-bye kiss.

"Promise us you'll be back," she whispered, tears dripping down her face.

"Girl, you're trippin'."

"Look at your daughter and promise her you'll be back."

Without saying a word, I kissed them both before heading out the front door.

Toi had been laid to rest at the cemetery on Martin Luther King Drive. When I reached her plot, I kneeled on the grass and laid my head against her headstone. I had the bottle of Henny clutched in my hand. I had drunk half of it on the drive over to the cemetery while listening to Faith Evan's *Missing You.*

With teary eyes I said, "Sis, I miss you like crazy. You was always my favorite girl. No matter what, in my eyes you could do no wrong. I would give anything for you to still be here with me. With you gone, life just ain't worth living." I took a gulp of Henny straight to the head. "Really, shawdy, I'm ready to join you. Like Pac said, 'fuck the world!' I cried. "But I gotta get the nigga who took you away from me. Yeah, I know that fuck ass nigga, Rich Kid, did it. I'ma serve his ass, that's my word! Damn, girl…" I sobbed, cutting my words short and swallowing my pain down with another sip.

My heart ached. I knew that I was the cause of Toi's murder. Through my tears, I saw an old lady placing flowers on a grave nearby. Toi's plot was decorated with lots of fresh flowers.

Mama must've been here recently.

I sat on the ground with my back against Toi's headstone and reminisced about our childhood, growing up in the projects and every single event we shared. Amazingly, we never fought. It had always been us against the world, making the pain of losing her was so intense.

"Fuck this shit!"

I downed the last bit of Henny, then I pulled my burner from my waist and locked one in the chamber.

Just as I raised the gun to my head, I heard, "No, boo. We need you." My head snapped around toward the voice.

Inez was standing to my side with Tamia in her arms.

I let my arm fall to my side, dropping the gun on the ground. Inez sunk to her knees next to me, handed me Tamia and then wrapped her arms around the both of us.

CHAPTER 16

Main man," said Murder Mike. We were at one of the stash houses counting loot. "You gotta regain your focus. All of the Dreads will be in town next weekend to discuss basing you in St. Louis with Rohan."

"Whatever, dawg." I was tired of the game.

I'd walk away before I'd moved to Missouri to help one of the Dreads do what he should've been able to do himself. Like I said before, my loyalty wasn't to the Dreads. My loyalty was to Murder Mike.

A few days before the Dreads were due in town, I was chillin' at Lonnie's crib with him and Delina, smoking weed and drinking Courvoisier. Shotgun Pete arrived and he and I got a little rawed on some powder he had. Later, Kyree showed up. We spent the whole day blazing and talking.

The next day, the same shit. I didn't snort any powder 'cause I'd done too much of that shit lately. No matter what was on my mental plate, I wasn't trying to become a powder head.

By noon Saturday, all four Dreads had arrived at the stash house in Lithonia. Already Murder Mike and I had been there since that morning when Crazy Nine had arrived with a van full of weed and coke packed in boxes.

As always, when Crazy Nine brought our supply of drugs to one of the stash houses, he parked the van in the backyard and we unloaded the van, carrying the boxes into the house through the back door. I'd watch the street from a window while they counted the dope Crazy Nine had delivered, then Crazy Nine counted the money Murder was turning in. It would sometimes take hours since there was so much money to be counted.

If I noticed po-po or robbers approach the house, all I could do was yell to them because I was unarmed. Crazy Nine had patted me down to be sure, as usual, a policy the Dreads strictly enforced whenever he delivered drugs to us. He obviously didn't trust me because him and Murder Mike were still strapped.

By the time Rastaman arrived at the stash house, Murder and Crazy Nine had stacked all the pounds of weed and kilos of cocaine in the back rooms. The money was outside locked in the van.

We all greeted one another and sat down around the kitchen table to discuss business affairs.

Around six o'clock we all got hungry. Rastaman went with me to get some KFC and sodas. My pager went off while we waited inside KFC for our large order to be filled. I used the phone in the restaurant's doorway area to call back the number on my pager. By the time I got off the phone, our order had been filled. I was so hungry I dug into one of the buckets of chicken as I drove back to the stash house.

At the kitchen table the fast food was attacked in earnest while discussions continued.

An hour later, Murder Mike and Crazy Nine left to go somewhere, saying they'd be back in a half hour. The rest of us moved to the front room where we fired up ganja and the three Dreads took turns battling each other at video Ninja warfare.

I unlocked the front door, opened it and looked out into the dusk-dark evening. The secluded subdivision street was quiet and still. Except for a man and woman who strolled hand-in-hand, passing by. I nodded at the couple and they nodded back.

"Whud up, mon?" asked Rastaman, coming to the door to see who I was nodding to or what I was looking at.

"Nothing up, mon," I said, mimicking his accent. "Just getting fresh air."

He watched the couple's backs as they strolled leisurely down the quiet street. Satisfied that the couple didn't represent any threat, Rastaman put the .9mm back in the shoulder holster he was wearing. I hadn't even seen him take the gun out.

"Close the door, mon," he said as he returned to the video game.

I shut the door.

"Every'ting cool?" Rohan asked.

"Everything cool," I assured them. I went into the kitchen to search for some KFC.

Minutes later, I heard pandemonium erupt! The front door slammed into the wall.

"DEA! Don't fuckin' move! Get down on the floor! Get down on the fuckin' floor! Try it! Go ahead!"

A woman's voice said, "Spread your legs! Arms up above your head! Don't move, buddy! I'll blow your head off!"

"What's going on, mon?"

"Shut up! Spread your legs! We're Drug Enforcement Agents!"

"I'm coming out officers!" I yelled from the kitchen, not wanting to surprise them and get my head shot off. "I'm not armed. My hands are in the air."

Four heavily armed agents stood in the front room, with DEA emblazoned across their T-shirts. The bulk of bulletproof vests were visible beneath the T-shirts. DEA was also across the caps and windbreakers in bold yellow letters. There were three men and a woman. All four of them smiled as I slowly entered the front room with my hands above my head. The woman, Delina, silently handed me her .9mm and began cuffing the Dreads, one by one.

Lonnie and Delina were the couple that had strolled past the house earlier.

As planned, they'd gone around the corner, where Pete and Kyree waited in the car and changed into their DEA gear.

"Be careful. They all have guns." I said and then told Lonnie to stand over Rastaman while Delina cuffed his hands behind his back.

"Fa sho!"

Lonnie pressed the barrel of the street-sweeper against the back of Rastaman's head, who said something to the other Dreads in a language I couldn't understand.

"Anybody move, kill 'em!" I barked to discourage whatever Rastman might've said.

Shotgun Pete stood over Rohan, the shotgun trained down on him, daring the Dread to move. Kyree stood over Jamaican Rick, with the AK-47, which was what I usually preferred. After all three Dreads were cuffed, me and Delina taped their mouths.

"You die for this, mon!" Rohan said before I taped his mouth.

"Maybe," I allowed. "But you die first, mon."

I'd been planning this for a while, which was the only reason I had made peace with Shotgun Pete. I knew that Lonnie and I couldn't pull it off by ourselves, and Kyree wasn't experienced enough to trust him with our lives without Shotgun Pete. Certainly Delina wasn't. In fact, Lonnie hadn't wanted to use her, but Shotgun Pete convinced us all that a woman's presence would make the DEA disguise more legit. At least initially, which would be long enough to gain control of the house. I had told them that I wouldn't give them the signal, stepping out the front door until everyone inside of the house was in one room.

I'd also expected Crazy Nine and Murder Mike to be there. We'd expected gun play because Murder would recognize Lonnie, Shotgun Pete and Delina.

124

Our main advantage was a surprise attack. That was what I'd hoped. It had worked out even better that Murder Mike and Crazy Nine weren't there. We all knew how dangerous the plan would be, one of us could get killed. I expected the Dreads and Murder Mike to buck, which was why Lonnie hadn't wanted Delina involved, but Delina was game and said that if Lonnie got killed, she wanted to die at his side. Real Bonnie and Clyde shit. Still we planned for her to enter the house last and to back out if shots were fired. Shotgun Pete was to bring along a .357 automatic. We hoped he'd get to toss it to me if there was resistance, since I already knew Crazy Nine would search me and I wouldn't be strapped. A reality I didn't like but saw no way around.

Fuck it, I said while planning it. I was all in, do or die!

I knew Crazy Nine's routine when he delivered drugs. I just had to wait until all four of the Dreads came to Atlanta.

I'd been the one pushing for us to go get something to eat because I had to get to a phone and let Lonnie know for sure that we were at the house in Lithonia.

It hadn't been him paging me when my pager went off at KFC. It had been Inez, but I used it as the perfect opportunity to call Lonnie and 'em and let them know that we were at the house in Lithonia. I just told them to wait an hour or so for the sun to go down. The rest had been well-rehearsed.

Now, with the three Dreads handcuffed, duct taped and dragged into a backroom where Shotgun Pete and Delina guarded them, Lonnie, Kyree and me waited for Crazy Nine and Murder Mike to return to the house. I looked out the window, mentally hurrying Crazy Nine and Murder's return.

"Kyree! Pull the car behind the house so they won't see it when they return," I said. He left the car parked at the curb.

Kyree returned from moving the car and re-joined us while we waited. I was amazed but relieved that no neighbors had seen the fraudulent DEA agents entering the house. If they had, they might had become suspicious of the agents being inside for so long and would call the local police.

A stash house in a quiet, remote area offered privacy but it also left dealers vulnerable.

Growing impatient, I told Kyree to begin loading some of the marijuana and cocaine into the car. "Fill up the trunk and the back seat."

"The back seat?" he asked.

"Yeah, Don't worry, a few of us will ride back in either the van or the truck they're in."

Twenty minutes later, I silently motioned Kyree to the front door as he walked back through the kitchen, having returned through the back door for another arm-load of dope. "Shhh!" I put my finger to my lips. "Here they come." I said in a harsh whisper.

As soon as Murder Mike and Crazy Nine entered through the front door, me, Lonnie and Kyree drew down on them, pushing them to the floor and quickly closing the front door.

"Move a muscle and I'ma pump some hot shit in y'all head!" I threatened.

"This how you do it?" spat Murder Mike.

"Homie, you ain't seen nothin' yet!" I spat back.

While Lonnie and Kyree trained their heat on the two, I searched their waist and removed their weapons.

"Fam, you're dead ass wrong for this!" said Murder Mike.

I dismissed his rebuke. "Say another word and I'ma show you *wrong* fa real! Now, both of y'all get the fuck up and act like y'all know we'll murder some shit!"

We yanked them to their feet and led them at gunpoint back into the room where Shotgun Pete and down-ass Delina held their comrades. Crazy Nine and Murder glared violently at me.

"Looks don't kill but I do," I said, shoving Murder Mike forward.

Once inside the back bedroom, all hell broke loose. Crazy Nine fell to the floor next to Rohan, rolled over and came up blasting. He'd had a small gun in an ankle holster. All of us blasted at him in unison, blowing five different size holes in the crazy Dread. I was worried that neighbors had definitely heard the short but loud burst of gunfire.

Shit!

Lonnie had been shot in the shoulder, and a bullet had grazed Delina's face where blood ran down.

Fuck!

Kyree was slumped down against the wall by the door, a hole in the center of his forehead. There was no doubt he was dead or if he wasn't, there was nothing we could do to save him. One of Crazy Nine's desperate shots had hit him right between the eyes.

I kept my heater trained on Murder Mike, who was still lying face-down on the floor with the others, while I told Pete to check Crazy Nine's pocket for the keys to the van.

I grabbed a pillow off the bed and covered the back of Murder's head with it. Then I pressed the gun against the pillow.

"It ain't personal, main man," I said in the same tone he used with me after I'd gotten out of the hospital with a broken jaw. "It's just business!"

With nothing to lose, he tried to wiggle from beneath the pillow with my knee in his back. But my trigger finger was instant.

Blocka! Blocka! Blocka!

The pillow muffled the sound of the .9mm and a pool of blood quickly formed on the carpet beneath and around my main man's head.

I could've let Murder Mike live. With the Dreads dead, I doubt he would've come after me, but I wasn't about to underestimate him like he'd done me. I knew those platinum fingernails of his were real. That still wasn't why I murked him, though. I put three in the back of his head because, as far as I was concerned, his fingers were wrapped around the lead pipe that broke my jaw. If the nigga really had hood love for me, he would've stepped to me with the real, before he went along with the Dreads' intimidation tactics. But he'd chosen sides. Now he lay at the sides he'd chosen. Real hood justice!

Lonnie and Delina were both bleeding. I told them to go start the car and wait for me and Shotgun Pete. As soon as they left the room, I used another pillow to execute all three handcuffed Dreads the same way I'd done Murder Mike. I hadn't wanted Shotgun Pete to use the shotgun, it was too noisy.

"Let's go!" I said to Pete.

He turned to leave the room just as I shot him in the back of the head.

He fell on his face, body twitching. Another shot to the back of the head stopped that. I snatched the van keys from his dead man's grip and ran outside to the van to get the duffle bag of money I knew Crazy Nine had locked inside. I hated leaving behind so much dope in the house, but there was no way to get the rest because both Lonnie and his lady were bleeding and, for all I knew, the police were on the way.

I tossed the duffel bag in the back seat on top of several boxes of dope.

"Scoot over!" I said to Delina.

I hopped in the driver's seat, squishing Delina over and against Lonnie's injured shoulder.

"Ahhh!" he yelped.

I had to drive on the grass to get around Murder's whip parked in the driveway, but I did so in a hurry and with no difficulty.

"Where's Pete?" Lonnie asked, obviously in pain.

"I left him with the others."

"Huh?"

"I left him with the others," I repeated. "I figured he couldn't be trusted. Besides, I owed him that."

The car was now leaving the subdivision. Inside of the van was complete silence. Maybe Lonnie and Delina were stunned by my revelation that I'd murked Shotgun Pete. But murking his punk-ass hadn't been spontaneous on my part, I'd known the whole time while planning the deadly robbery that I was gonna blast Pete before we left out that stash house. He was a fool to believe that the beef had genuinely been squashed. He should've known that if we had beef one day, we would still have beef the next. The only mafucka who can get money with and forgive a nigga who had crossed him was a fake nigga who'd cross his man himself. Trill niggaz weren't built like that. We loved hard and hated harder.

Not hate as in being jealous of a nigga. I was speaking of a strong despise of the enemy. *What? I'ma help a nigga come up who has done me a serious bad? Never!*

At Lonnie's crib, I left everything in the vehicle but the duffel bag as we went inside to check the extent of their wounds. Delina's face had almost stopped bleeding, her injury was superficial. The wound to Lonnie's shoulder was more serious. After Delina cleaned it up, we could see where the bullet had gone straight through.

"That is much better than if the bullet had lodged in his shoulder," Delina said.

Lonnie was still in pain and we couldn't stop the bleeding. We all knew we couldn't take him to the hospital. They would've called the police, as is their policy for all gunshot victims, no matter how minor the injury.

Lonnie remembered that he knew a veterinarian, who smoked weed and snorted a little cocaine. He said he met the dude through Shotgun Pete, but he didn't know the vet's office or home phone number and could only vaguely recall where the vet had said his office was located.

Anyway, it was nighttime now and the vet wouldn't be at the office this late. All we could do was keep Lonnie's wound cleaned and wrapped and feed my dawg extra-strength Tylenols until morning.

CHAPTER 17

Delina located the veterinarian early next morning and for a few grand and a half kilo of cocaine, he patched up Lonnie's shoulder and sent him to a friend's pharmacy for pain pills.

We'd split the bounty sixty-forty. I kept sixty percent of the money and drugs we'd taken and Lonnie and his lady shared the remainder.

My plan was to sell my kilos to niggaz I'd met while rolling as Murder Mike's bodyguard. We hadn't taken that much weed because cocaine was more valuable. The money from the caper went with my stash. What Lonnie and Delina planned to do with theirs was their own business.

After I sold all the dope, my plans were to retire from crime and take a minute to figure out what I wanted to do with the rest of my life. I wasn't sure if I wanted to remain in Atlanta or not. I was thinking of moving away, maybe looking Juanita up, but she would have to be willing to accept Inez. There was no way I was cutting Inez off. She had held a nigga down like a real trooper.

Toi's death had taken a lot out of a nigga. It had made me realize that no matter how careful I was, those that I loved and cared for remained vulnerable to my enemies. I did not want to go away and leave any of my children sitting ducks for Rich Kid's revenge. Although I'd never known him to go after an enemy's children, I didn't know for sure he wouldn't. So whatever I did, I'd have to move my seeds away with me. Of course Shan would never consent to me taking Lil' T.

Speaking of Shan, two days after the caper, she began calling Lonnie, asking where Shotgun Pete was. Lonnie told Shan that he hadn't seen Pete, but Shan didn't believed him.

According to Lonnie, Shan said that Shotgun Pete had told her about the hit on the Dreads. Now Shan was worried because Pete hadn't called. He'd been missing for two days. The massacre inside of the house in Lithonia, miraculously remained undiscovered. Whenever the discovery was made, I knew it would be all over the news and the streets would be aflame with gossip and accusations. Fingers would automatically point at me since I was still standing. Shan would probably scream names once Pete's body was discovered and identified. I didn't think for a minute that the skank bitch would spare me because I was the father of her son. Cita would probably scream, too, now that her free ride to high living was deceased.

Shit!

I hadn't anticipated stupid-ass Pete telling Shan about our plans. She could definitely point the po-po down the right trail. Lonnie and Delina's blood had no doubt been left at the scene, probably dripped all the way from the backroom to the backyard. My fingerprints were everywhere inside of the house, too.

Shan had to die. Point blank period!

We agreed that Lonnie was to murk Shan. He could easily get her to meet him on the premise that Pete had sent a message by him. If I had asked her to meet me, she'd be suspicious because I never wanted to see her unless it was to pick up my son. I could've used that ploy but then I would've had to murk the bitch in front of our son. Nah, I wasn't that cold. Anyway, Lonnie said he'd handle it.

In the meantime, I was selling keys cheap, just trying to get rid of the shit, stash the loot and *vroom!* I knew now that my future was not in the ATL. I had prepared Inez for the likelihood that I might have to bounce with no warning, I couldn't tell her what had gone down, nor did she ask, which was true to her ways.

Lonnie hadn't slumped Shan yet, and I knew that the bitch was going to be a problem once the shit hit the fan, so I set out to do what had to be done, even though I had conflicting emotions about it. Not that I had any love for Shan, that was dead. But I did have love for Poochie, and I loved Lil' T to no end. Murking Shan would definitely hurt them, which I didn't wanna do. On the other hand, I believed that leaving her alive would come back to haunt me.

Self-preservation, I thought, the *law of the land.*

Little did I realize, at the time, how very true those words would turn out to be.

I climbed through the window of the apartment, almost losing the wig that I was wearing. Once inside, I straightened the wig on my head and slipped the burner out of my waist.

It was three am, so no one was outside of the complex. I was sure that I had entered the apartment unnoticed.

The apartment was dark and quiet, but I'd been there numerous times to pick my son up, so I was familiar with the layout. I crept through the kitchen and eased to the stairs, which led upstairs to the bedroom. When I reached the top of the stairs, I saw light shining under the bottom of the closed bathroom door. The lights appeared to be off in the two bedrooms.

I twisted a silencer on my Glock as I tip-toed to Shan's bedroom door. Just as I touched the doorknob, I heard a noise behind me! I spun around, ready to blast.

"Hey, Daddy!" said Lil' T, rubbing sleep from his eyes. "Why you got on a wig?"

"Shhh! I put a finger to my lips whispering, "I was just playin' a trick on your mama. Go on back to bed."

"Okay. I had to pee. Is you gon' spend the night?"

"Nah, I gotta go. Don't tell your mama I was here, okay?"

"Okay, Daddy," Lil' T promised, staring at the gun in my hand.

I sent him back to bed without further explanation. I damn sure wasn't going to explain to him that he had just saved his mama's life.

A week after we completed the hit at the stash house, the bodies were finally discovered. Neighbors had telephoned the police, complaining about the foul odor emitting from the residence.

"After police discovered the massacre," the reporter said, *"a neighbor who declined to be on camera recalled hearing what sounded like gunshots one night, almost a week ago."*

From that moment on, shit went crazy.

Lonnie told me that Shan called him crying, wanting to know if Pete was one of the yet to be identified victims. She'd seen the news. Lonnie tried talking Shan into meeting him, under the pretense of taking her to where Pete was hiding out. Shan agreed to meet Lonnie but not at night and not anywhere where there wouldn't be other people. It was obvious that Shan did not trust Lonnie. Perhaps Shotgun Pete had told her something that made her leery of meeting him.

Lonnie said Shan wouldn't agree to meet him at any of the places he'd suggested.

Poochie hadn't raised no fool for a daughter. Shan got ghost all of a sudden. Now she wasn't even answering her cell phone when Lonnie called, and no one was at her apartment.

That night, the news station identified all seven victims of the drug-related massacre. I told Lonnie that the time had come for us to leave Atlanta. If Pete had told Shan what was supposed to go down, we couldn't trust the bitch not to scream on us. She'd probably blame us for Pete being killed, might even suspect me.

I was moving fast, getting shit in order to bounce far away. I told Inez I'd send for her once I touched down somewhere and felt it was safe for her to join me. My plan was to get ghost in about three days. I accelerated those plans when Lonnie paged me and said all of our pictures—his, Delina's and mine were on the news and police had listed us as suspects.

No one had to tell me that the police had been to any and every place I'd ever lived or hung out looking for me. They had surely done that before putting my old mug shot on television, knowing I'd disappear after that.

What helped me elude arrest, even without knowing the cops were already looking for me, was that I wasn't laying low at Inez' crib nor was I being seen in the streets. No one knew where my crib was plus I hardly stayed there. And Lonnie and Delina hadn't been staying at either of their cribs.

I had to move fast.

I called Keisha from a payphone on Old National Highway.

"Hey, baby! I'm so worried about you." Tears were in her voice.

"I'm a'ight, shawdy. I need you to meet me."

"Okay, where?"

"At Ryan's on Old National."

"I'm on my way."

"Keisha, come by yourself."

"Nigga, you ain't gotta tell me that. I'm on point."

Twenty minutes later, I saw Keisha pull into the parking lot in her Yukon Denali with the tinted windows. I wasn't worried about being setup. I knew that lil' mama could be trusted. She was ride-or-die.

I slid into the passenger seat and closed the door.

"What's up, shawdy?"

"Nigga, they got y'all all on the news! You gonna be okay, baby? You need my help? Just gimme the game plan and I'm down with whateva."

135

"Shawdy, I'm 'bout to get ghost. But check this, I got about one hundred twenty-five bricks and fifty pounds of weed in storage down the street." I reached in my pocket. "Here's the key," I said, handing it to her. "The storage is in a fake name but hurry up and get that shit out of there just in case the po-po stumbles up on it and links it to me."

"What do you want me to do with it?"

"Do *you*, lil' mama. All I ask is that you bless Inez. She'll bless my Ma Dukes and my son."

"Okay."

"Don't let me down, Keisha."

"Nigga, if you didn't trust a bitch, you wouldn't be sittin' in my truck with the whole Atlanta police force lookin' for your ass. Don't worry, I'ma handle mines. Will *you* be okay, though?"

"No doubt," I assured her. "But when my time comes, you know I'm goin' out like a G."

I hugged Keisha and then said, "Shawdy, take flight on those niggaz in the game. Don't let Angel turn you straight veggie."

"Neva," she vowed, squeezing my dick through my pants. "Can I get some of this before you bounce?"

"Naw, shawdy," I laughed, "a nigga gotta jet."

I hugged her one last time, then I slid out of her ride.

I gave Lonnie the phone number where he could call Inez at work if he needed to get a message to me.

"I'll call her every so often to see if you've contacted her," I said. "Just be sure to call from a pay phone. They may have her home phone tapped, eventually, but not her work phone."

"Can we trust her, dawg?" worried Lonnie.

"No doubt," I tried to assure him.

"You're positive?"

"Trust my judgment, tight man." Then I told him what Inez had helped me do. That shit with King in Kentucky.

Lonnie said, "I guess she's solid, then. Where you gon' go? You thought about that yet?"

"Probably to Nevada, Juanita is out there."

He told me he was taking Delina and the kids up to New York.

"I'll be in touch through Inez when I get where I'm going," he promised. "Stay real, nigga. Much love," said Lonnie.

"You do the same, tight man," I said sincerely. "If we never see each other again, you still gon' be a nigga's heart, dawg. You the realest nigga I know. Much love. Tell Delina I said the same."

"Lay low, nigga."

"I'm out."

Ca$h

CHAPTER 18

Nevada felt like an oven even though it was past summer. Sweat from my forehead ran down past my brow getting under the leather eye patch and into my eye. The eye-patch, along with a short haircut, was just another measure I'd taken to change my appearance from the old mug shot pictures of me that the police had. It wasn't much of a disguise but it was all I could think of.

The long ride on the Ninja I'd purchased a few days before I'd left Atlanta had been tiresome, but a nigga on the run had to do what he had to do.

I had made the journey with a fake ID and driver's license, a backpack full of big face Benjamin's and two loaded nines, with extra clips. The backpack of loot was mostly hundreds and fifties, enough to last a while, so I wouldn't have to chance going back to my stash in Atlanta any time soon. Plus, the compartment under the bike's seat was full of hundred-dollar bill stacks. The bike had a temporary tag on it, which wasn't traceable to me because I'd used the fake ID when purchasing it from the Kawasaki dealership.

I'd left my whips parked in the driveway of the crib. Them po-po mafuckaz could have all that shit whenever they found it. None of it meant anything to me now.

I knew they would never find my money stash in Atlanta. I'd hidden it well. I'd go back for it one day, maybe in a few years.

I understood I might never see any of my children again. The cops would keep them under surveillance along with Inez and my mother, expecting me to try to contact or visit them. That's how fugitives always got caught, returning to visit family or a girlfriend. I wasn't going out like that.

I loved my seeds, cared for Inez deeply and if I overlooked my anger, I loved my Ma Dukes. But I wasn't ever returning to

Atlanta unless it was to get the rest of my stash or to murk Rich Kid if he ever resurfaced.

Maybe one day Inez and Tamia could slip away and come to me, but even that would be too risky. I knew for sure I wouldn't see my son again because I most definitely couldn't contact Shan. She'd probably pointed the cops in our direction.

It was a bitter pill for me to swallow, having to accept I'd never get to see Lil' T and Tamia again. The alternative was going back to see them and ending up in prison forever, which was no alternative at all.

With a little help from convenient store attendants in Las Vegas, I found the address Juanita had written on a sheet of blue stationary. I didn't have a phone number for her, so I couldn't call and let her know to be expecting me.

More than a year had passed since I'd seen Juanita. She could've moved again or had a man living with her. Or she might've heard I was wanted and might slam the door in my face. If either was the case, I'd hop back on my bike and head on to some small city in California.

No. A large city, where I could get lost in the crowd. Mafuckaz in small places were nosy and suspicious, especially of a young nigga wearing a leather eye-patch.

I pulled up in front of the apartment that matched the address on the stationary paper, parked the bike and took off my helmet and the eye patch. I left the seat compartment locked. The backpack on my back. I knocked on the door.

No answer.

The evening sun beamed on the back of my neck.

Then, "Who's there?" The west coast hadn't changed that sweet sounding voice.

"Youngblood."

"Who?"

"Youngblood," I repeated.

The door swung open. A look of surprise. Her eyes blinked like she was making sure it wasn't a dream. Then a huge beautiful smile appeared on her face. She was wearing the diamond-crusted inter-locking hearts pin I'd given her. No other jewelry, unless I counted the hand-woven plastic-string necklace and pendant that hung around her neck. The pendant caught my eye because it looked like a religious symbol: an eight-point star with a number seven in the middle.

In an instance I thought: *Has shawdy turned into a religious nut? Is that why she moved away? To follow the Lord? Shit! God already stole Poochie from a nigga.*

Juanita's arms went around me. "Hi, baby! What are you doing way out here?" Not really a question, mostly surprised.

"Am I still welcomed?"

"Of course you are!" Finally releasing me from her feminine bear hug.

"Oh, excuse my manners. Please come in! I'm so excited to see you."

The inside of the apartment was much cooler than the sweltering heat at my back. I followed Juanita into a small living room where three men and a gorgeous dark skinned shawdy sat on the floor, on pillows, in a circle. An unoccupied pillow must've been where Juanita had been sitting before I interrupted their little party. I quickly scanned the dudes, wondering which was Juanita's boyfriend. The bitch was wearing the inter-locking hearts pin I'd given to her to remember a nigga, while entertaining her nigga and some friends.

That's a bitch for you!

"Look, I'll stop by later," I said at her heels. "I didn't know you had company." I felt a twinge of jealously but mostly I didn't want her friends to see my face and remember it if my mug popped up on *America's Most Wanted*. I held my head down as much as possible without looking retarded.

"No, no, no, you better not dare leave!" Juanita took my hand in hers.

"These are my people." She turned to the group who had all stood up.

"Pardon self. This is a close friend of mine from Atlanta." I cringed. "His name is—"

"Popeye!" I cut her off, squeezing her hand as a signal to let the lie stand.

She introduced a tall, skinny, real dark dude as Wise Professor. He looked to be forty years old. A medium-height, brown-skin nigga with a bald head was named Intelligent Knowledge Allah. That's how she introduced him.

"Just call me Intelligent," dude said and dapped hands with me.

The third dude was, "Born Conscious Soldier," Juanita said.

I dapped dude's hand, too, wondering what type of good-good these fools were on.

Do all people in Vegas name their kids crazy shit like this?

I braced myself for the chocolate honey's name.

"And this is Asia." Cool. That was a simple enough name.

"Pleased to meet you." Her voice was strong, but pleasant. Her handshake firm, but feminine. She reminded me of Lauren Hill who used to be with the Fugees.

The dude, Wise Professor, said to Juanita: "Queen Africa, we'll continue building next week."

"Okay. At Intelligent's place, right?"

"Right," he confirmed.

I remained in the small living room while Juanita, Queen Africa, walked her company to the door.

From the living room I heard: "Peace."

"See you in school Wednesday. Peace."

"Peace, God."

"Peace, Earth."

I was sitting on the couch when Juanita returned to the living room.

"So, what brings you all the way to Nevada?" She stacked the floor pillows neatly in a corner. I waited until she was done and came and sat next to me, before I responded.

I told her that I'd gotten into some serious trouble and had to leave Atlanta, for good. For her own good, in case I was ever arrested, I didn't tell her what I'd done. I did let her know that I was wanted by police and told her not to be surprised if one day she saw pictures of me on television. I lied, telling her that I wasn't guilty of the crimes I was wanted for, but I had no way to prove my innocence.

"If you want me to leave, I will." I tried to read her eyes.

Could she be trusted not to call 911 the minute I turned my back? Was she on some religious trip, a devout Muslim or something, that would demand that she turn me in? What did the eight-point star hanging from the string around her neck mean? I had to believe that it was more than something worn as an accessory. Like the necklace, it had to stand for something to her.

Fuck it!

If Juanita sold me out to po-po I had two fully-loaded nine-millimeters with two fully-loaded extra clips. My peeps wouldn't be the only mafuckaz dressed in black, crying over a grave!

"Are you hungry?" asked Juanita.

"Nah, I'm cool?"

"Would you like a soda?" she offered. "That's all I have to drink. I don't drink alcoholic beverages. Oh, I have bottled water?"

I declined.

"So, you're never going back to Atlanta?"

"Not for a long time. If I do go back, it'll just be to get the money I left there."

"Am I to assume you plan on staying with me? Or is this just a brief stop before you head elsewhere?"

"I was kinda hoping I was welcomed here, with you," I said.

"You are." Her response was quick. Sincere. She unconsciously fingered the pin above her left breast. Or maybe she did it consciously.

"But, I don't want to stay here in this apartment," I clarified.

Juanita let out a small laugh. "Oh, you don't like my little place, huh? I forgot, you're used to much more luxury."

"It ain't that, shawdy. I just don't wanna take a chance on living in an apartment so close to neighbors who may see my picture on TV and recognize me."

"Is it really that bad, whatever the reason you had to leave Atlanta?" asked Juanita.

I just nodded.

That night Juanita slept in her bedroom, the only one in the small apartment. I slept fitfully on the couch, both loaded gats under the pillow Juanita had given me off of her bed. I dreamt of Inez, my children and all that I'd left behind in ATL.

I gave Juanita twenty-five hundred to give to the apartment manager to legally let her out of the lease agreement she'd recently renewed. We moved into a newly-built tract house in East Las Vegas, in a middle-class neighborhood, nothing fancy that would draw attention to a young couple.

The house was damn near identical to every other one on the street that lead to the cul-de-sac where ours was located.

There were only five houses on the cul-de-sac. Juanita said the four other houses were owned by middle-aged or old couples. Which was good *and* bad.

The differences in our ages would keep our neighbors from trying to get too friendly with us. On the other hand, old people were nosy and loved cop shows. I'd wear the eye patch and a cap whenever leaving the house and never be outside in the yard or driveway long enough for the old mafuckaz to get a good look at me.

As for the friends who'd been at Juanita's apartment when I first arrived there, Juanita explained that her people were Gods, and Asia was Conscious Soldier's Earth. And even if any of them ever did see my picture on TV, they would never turn me in to the devils and make me face the white man's justice.

"Which is really injustice," she said. "Because the court system is ruled by the white man and his laws, designed to function as another form of genocide."

"Huh?" I was lost.

I had been locked up with some Five-Percenters during the five-year bid I served, but I never had interest in it.

Juanita explained that she was a Five-Percenter and what it meant. Islam was her way of life, *not* a religion or a belief. She was *not* a Muslim, definitely not a Christian and not an atheist.

"I don't believe in God, not the mystery creation the white man inflicts upon us. In fact, I don't believe in anything. I either know it or I don't know it," she explained. "And the only God I know is the black man."

She told me that Wise Professor was her enlightener and that he and the others I'd met were also Five Percenters. They'd been building together the night I had shown up at her door.

"Building what, shawdy?" I asked. And felt foolish when she explained what she'd meant by building.

"I'm not going to trip on you calling me shawdy." she said, "'Cause I know you're not conscious. But hopefully one day you'll become conscious and see me and other black women for the Earths we are. Though I'll be the first to admit that most of us don't know our true essence ourselves."

I was hearing Juanita, but I wasn't really feeling what she was stressing. It sounded like she was on some Queen Latifah or Sister Souljah shit—two bitches that didn't seem to wanna accept that a nigga was the couch, the female was the rug, always beneath us. Never equal or on top. Not to a real nigga!

It was time to put the dick in Juanita and make her bow down before this Queen shit Wise Professor was teaching got embedded in her head. I'd make her get on her knees and give a nigga some brain, my way of letting her know she'd always be looking up to me!

It wasn't that I wasn't feeling Juanita. She was still sweet and attentive to me. I just needed to lay down the law. I couldn't live with Queen Latifah the rest of my life.

I'd been in Las Vegas four weeks, had spent every night in the same house with Juanita, some nights in the same bed, yet I hadn't sexed her since my arrival. I'd tried two or three times, but Juanita had rebuffed a nigga, saying she wanted me to be certain that it was more than just sex I wanted and that she wasn't gon' come home from school one day and find me gone.

"If it ever goes down like that," I'd assured her, "it'll be because po-po was hot on my ass."

Sitting around the house all day long, doing nothing but watching television and playing video games was hard for a nigga like me to get used to. I was used to pushing fly whips and gettin' at bitches all day. Now I was living like a hermit or an old man.

I'd given Juanita the money to go out and buy me mad shit to keep me entertained in the house while she was at school or somewhere building with her people. Still I was bored to death. I had no transportation while Juanita was gone. But that was by design. If I never drove a car, I didn't have to worry about being pulled over for a traffic violation and being detained and maybe fingerprinted because of the fake ID I carried.

I'd rode the Ninja to a mostly Mexican section of West Las Vegas, parked it, left it with the keys in the ignition, got in the Cressida with Juanita and forgot about the bike. It was probably in Tijuana by now.

Some days the crazy urge to go out and buy a fly whip, mad bling and mad gear and cruise the West Vegas hoods for some fine Mexican cha cha was almost overwhelming.

The casinos and bright lights of the Vegas strip were also tempting. Surely I could blend in with the crowd on the strip. Before I had come out to Las Vegas, I thought the whole city was casinos, hotels, and other tourist spots. I knew UNLV was in Vegas, too, but I never thought there were regular neighborhoods like in any other city. Grocery stores, hospitals, fast food restaurants, the whole nine. I wanted to experience the whole city, especially the casinos and the Mexican and Mexican/black bitches—the cha cha!

A fly whip and crazy jewels would make it all easily accessible. What good was having crazy, stupid loot if I couldn't go out and enjoy it? That's what tugged at me when I was bored, but my better senses kept me from doing some stupid shit that might get me popped and extradited back to the ATL to face *the devil's injustice,* as Juanita would say.

Just when the boredom seemed to broaden, Juanita lightened my mood with a sumptuous dinner. She cooked broiled lobster and shrimp, broccoli, corn on the cob and sour dough bread. She never ate anything fried but would fry chicken and other meats for me, if I asked her. Tonight's meal was a'ight, though. She had some type of bottled water with her meal. I had Old English with mine.

After dinner she cleaned the dishes, and we moved into the den where Juanita usually studied for two hours, as was her routine. I put on my headphones, plugged them into the big flat screen as not to disturb her, and watched Monday Night Football. I'd usually put on headphones and listen to music, read a magazine or the newspaper while she studied, unless a game was on I wanted to see. I'd asked her if being in the den while she was studying bothered her.

"Not at all," she said, smiling sweetly. "Matter of fact, I concentrate better just having you in the room with me."

Juanita closed the thick textbook, sat it on the end table and took off her sporty reading glasses. She folded her legs up-under her Indian style and watched me watch the game. She had to be watching me and not the game 'cause every time I looked at her she was looking at me.

"Whud up?"

"Nothing. I just like looking at you." Smiling

"You trippin'," I said.

"You trippin'," Juanita said, imitating my voice.

"Oh, you're finished studying and now you wanna play?" I tossed a pillow at her. When she caught it, I tackled her like a linebacker.

"Okay! Okay!" she huffed when I let her up. "Now it's on!" She tossed me the pillow. "You run the ball. C'mon!"

I went into my running back role, but let Juanita tackle me to the floor.

"Who's the baddest?" she taunted on top of me.

"I am," I said.

She stood up and came crashing down on me with an elbow, WWF style.

"Owww!" I yelped. "You the baddest!" I conceded.

She moved to let me up but I held onto her and kissed her on the mouth. Her lips were as soft as usual and receptive. Soon our tongues were deliciously tangled. My hands caressed her back, went under her T-shirt and unsnapped her bra. Her breasts were full like I remembered them. I felt her quiver. I lifted her shirt and covered a nipple with my lips. I sucked it gently. Her hands were on the back of my head, encouraging me to continue. I flicked the nipple with my tongue. She panted. I felt her body heating up. My hands went down her body and underneath the elastic of her shorts and cupped her butt. With my middle finger I felt her wetness. Lying on top of me she had to feel my hardness pressing between her legs.

"I wanna make love to you," I whispered in her ear.

"Why?" she whispered back. "Tell me why you want me."

Shit! What kind of question was that? Couldn't she feel that I was rock hard? That was *why* I wanted her!

Juanita must've sensed that I was struggling to verbalize an answer but what nigga could think with a hard dick? She gave me a quick kiss on the lips and then got up and fixed her clothes properly, except for her bra, which she took off without removing her T-shirt, a magic trick I could never figure out how women did it. They had to have been taught it 'cause every one of 'em could do it.

She handed me a notebook tablet and a pen. "I want to make love to you, too," Juanita said, "I haven't slept with anyone since we were together more than two years ago."

"You want me to believe that?" I couldn't help asking.

"Believe what you like. The truth remains the truth regardless whether you know it or not. Anyway, hush." She put her finger to my lips. "We'll make it meaningful and fun," continued Juanita. "I'm going to go bathe. While I'm away getting fresh and perfumed, you write down why you want to make love to me. No lies just to make me feel good. I don't need that. Then I'll write down why I want to make love to you, while you bathe and get cologned. Then we can read what each other wrote before we make love." Her lips pressed against mine. "No lies or games." Her finger jabbed the air in front of my face, but a pretty smile accompanied the warning.

Off to bathe she went.

I stared at the blank paper until I heard Jill *Scott's Do You Remember Me?* playing on the system that we'd had wired to play from wall speakers in every room throughout the house. Jaunita must've turned it on from the bedroom. I was feeling Jill Scott, so I turned off the football game and began to write.

I wanna make love to you, shawdy, because I do remember you. Meaning I remember how it felt the last time we made love a long, long, time ago. Since then, I've done a lot of things and met many females, but I always had memories of you. Juanita, you know I'm not no poet, so I don't have any clever words or verses to describe how you make a nigga feel. All I can say is, I wanna make love to you because you're the only woman I've ever made love to. The others were just sex. I say that because I never thought about them when we weren't in bed. With you it's different. It wasn't just a physical thing. You made me feel something that I thought I could never feel. And I still feel that for you, whether we make love tonight or not. Whether we ever make love again! Mostly though, I wanna make love to you to show you what I feel but cannot say...

"Time's up," announced Juanita as she came into the den wrapped in only a towel that covered her breasts down to her mid-thighs. "I've already drawn a tub of water for your bath, just the way you like it."

I pulled her to me and kissed her. Jill Scott was singing a different song by now but a nice one, still.

Juanita was first to break the kiss. "Now go, so I can write." She nudged me toward the bathroom.

The bath water was hot and soothing. I sank down further in the tub so that all but my head was submerged underneath. I heard Jill Scott stop in mid-song, then Musiq Soulchild started crooning *Love*. Probably from the same CD I'd given Juanita before she left Atlanta after her mom's funeral.

I closed my eyes and listened to his lyrics—ideas that sounded good on CD but were, thus far, foreign to me. However, Juanita made a nigga feel like she was the type of female Musiq Soulchild was spittin' about in the song.

When I walked into the den in nothing but boxers, freshly bathed, cologne-splashed, Juanita was through writing. Still clad in only a towel, she looked sexy and definitely eatable sitting on the couch. Mad thigh was showing me that underneath the towel was nothing but naked pleasure. Musiq Soulchild was crooning the same song over and over, but from the expression on Juanita's face, it was all good.

We took our papers back into the master bedroom, where I laid across the queen-size bed while Juanita lotioned my body and nibbled on my earlobes. She changed the music from Soulchild to instrumental jazz, then she handed me what she had written. I handed her my paper and told her it contained no lies or games.

"Promise?"

"No doubt," I said and we both began reading.

Juanita had written:

I want to make love with you tonight for the same reason I chose to make love with you once before and for the same reason I haven't been with anyone since. Because I believe it is "love" that we made that night, and not just an act to satisfy passion. I don't give myself to passion, I give myself to love. I know what I had begun to feel for you before I gave myself to you last time, and that feeling continued to blossom even when we were apart. I love you. Yes! I LOVE YOU! Understand that, okay? Although that love is in its early stages, it is real love, nevertheless. By sharing love with you, I know I'll help you learn to show the love that is buried deep inside of you. The love that all gods possess for their earths.

You are the sun. I am the moon. Though you're not conscious of it, you are the foundation of all things in existence, including me. When you come to know yourself, I will receive my light from you. Tonight I want to receive your tenderness. I want to feel your touch and give you mine 'cause I know that it will just be the beginning of a love that will be ours forever. So tonight, I will not be timid or shy. I will try to please you and help you to feel what you make me feel. Tonight I will give you all of me, baby. It was almost 2 ½ years ago, but I remember that night like it was just yesterday. So, tonight we build on yesteryear. We build on today. WE BUILD ON FOR ALWAYS...

That night our love-making was slow and intense. Juanita was naturally small, but her inactive sex life had made her even tighter. I'd been patient and gentle, allowing her time to get used to my size. From there, our bodies became one.

Yeah, I know it's ill for a young G to be talking some Dave Hollister shit. On the real, though, I was feelin' like I was not only making love to Juanita, I was becoming a part of her and her a part of me. The shit fucked with my mental 'cause I didn't wanna feel like that about nobody!

Life was too fickle, especially for a nigga on the run. I had already lost every person I ever loved, my seeds and my fam'. Rich Kid's weak ass had murdered my sister 'cause he was too weak to bring it to me. Cheryl had got ghost with two of my lil' princesses, and I had to jet and leave Lil' T and Tamia behind, probably forever. Ma Dukes had sold me out, as far as I was concerned. I had love for my dawg Lonnie, but circumstances dictated that we remain ghost from each other. I had love for Murder Mike, but murked him 'cause he hadn't had real love for me. Inez I cared for, maybe loved, but she too was now lost to me. Our forced separation showed me just how much I really cared about her and how much I'd lost.

I wasn't trying to feel what Juanita was making a nigga feel. Life would not let it last. At any minute I might have to get ghost. Due to my situation, I was forced to live reclusively. That meant I seldom went outdoors, which denied Juanita the simple pleasures of companionship, like having her man with her to pick out groceries, or new household appliances, inviting friends from school over to study or discuss theories on whatever topics they discussed in class. For my comfort, she no longer held ciphers, sessions with her Five Percenter people at the crib. She still attended those weekly ciphers, but at one of the others crib.

Curious about the ideology, I'd ask her questions. Juanita was emphatic about the Five Percenter's teachings being the truth and not an idea or faith. She told me some shit, like, whenever I really wanted the truth, she would prove to me that the black man was indeed god. She said she'd let me build with Wise Professor, and he would help me see my true culture and that would give me power, which would bring me out of the triple stages of darkness.

She might as well have been speaking Chinese. I wasn't understanding or trying to understand that shit. I respected her convictions but my mind wasn't trying to share them. It wasn't a a problem, though, because Juanita never let it affect our chemistry.

Sometimes I'd go out at night, wearing the eye-patch, with Juanita to a movie or some other venture where it would be too dark for anyone to get a good look at me. Never to a restaurant or nightclub, Juanita loved the former, but had no interest in the latter. If my forced reclusiveness bothered Juanita, she never allowed its effects to show.

Baby girl showed unconditional love for a nigga, never hittin' emotional switches, flip flopping or any of that shit. We were like Will Smith and Jada.

CHAPTER 19

Juanita was behind the wheel of the Ford Explorer, with tinted bubble windows. I had given her the loot to put a down payment on it. I could've easily bought the SUV with cash, but I wasn't trying to draw any attention to shawdy. The Explorer wasn't tricked-out, no custom rims or DVD player. Just plain, like it was when it left the dealers lot, except for the tinted bubble windows. It gave me a better feeling of security because other motorist couldn't see inside like they could the Cressida.

It took about four hours to reach Los Angeles. We got there around five a.m., which meant it was eight o'clock back in Atlanta. Juanita found a payphone that I could use while still in the truck, then she went inside the store to give me privacy.

When Inez came to the phone, I said, "Good Morning. This is the gentleman who services your car." That was a pre-arranged code to let her know it was me calling.

"Hi!" Inez responded with what certainly was more excitement than one would be expected to have for their mechanic. Calming her voice, she said, "Thanks for calling, my car is running fine."

That told me it was safe to talk, or at least, Inez felt it was so. Had she had reason to think the call was being traced, she would've said her car was giving her trouble.

Her first words after that were, "I love you, boo. I miss you so much."

"Are you and Tamia, okay?"

"We're fine. She's getting bigger by the day. I tell her you love her every day." Her voice was full of emotion.

"That's good. Is the heat still on?"

"Like crazy. Watching my every move."

"You sure this phone is straight?"

"Yeah, it's straight."

"Any message from my tightman?"

"Two weeks ago. They're cool. Didn't say where they're at. Told me to tell you to be chill, much love."

"That's cool," I said. "Next time he hollas, tell him I'm good, and I'll check back in a few. Anyway, is it bad there, I mean, the news and shit?"

"Yeah. Real bad. Still in the papers." Her voice sounded sad for me. A little worried, too.

"I figured that," I told her. "Well, what's done is done. Fuck it. How you livin'?"

"Me and the kids are fine. You left us straight. Plus, I still got mine, and Keisha has been breaking me off. I wanna be with you, though."

"Not right now."

"I understand. Still I miss you."

"Somebody been sleepin' in my bed?"

"Me and Tamia and Bianca when she's acting jealous," Inez said.

"Right, right. What about the nigga you ain't telling me about?" I was just fuckin' with her.

"You the only nigga I want. You don't know that by now?"

I didn't answer right away. When I did, I said, "I don't know, shawdy. Time changes shit."

"Nigga, anyplace, anytime. You call it, I'll be there. Fuck everything and everybody else."

I said, "I know you would." Changing subjects, I said, "Hey, you seen my lil' man?"

"Nah, that mama of his ain't hearing that. I give money to Poochie for him, though. Shan be on some sideways shit."

"*Hmmph!* What about Rich Kid? He back in the city?"

"I haven't heard it. But, then again, I don't go anywhere. Oh, I moved."

"Yeah?"

"Uh-huh. Ann is worried about you."

"Just let her know I'm good, and tell her I said I love her, despite everything."

"Okay."

"I gotta go," I said. "I'll holla again, when I can."

"We love you."

"Remember that," I told her. Then I said good-bye.

I wiped the phone before reaching out the window and re-placing it on the hook. By the time Juanita returned to the whip, I was deep in thought, missing my seeds like crazy, wishing I could just hear their voices. Missing Inez, too, to be real about it. A nigga gotta have some love for a shawdy that's *that* down.

Juanita was down, too. In her own way. She drove back to Las Vegas, never complaining of being tired or asking who I'd called. She must've understood the logic of wanting to make the call far away from where we lived. And she didn't complain one time when I bumped rap CD's the whole ride back.

Juanita didn't have classes that day so she went straight to bed when we got back to the crib. I put some leftovers in the mi-crowave, waited for them to heat, then I took my grub into the den and popped in the DVD *Friday*. After the movie ended, I put in re-runs of the *Martin Lawrence* show and fired up a fat stogie filled with some of that good Mexican weed that Juanita got for me.

My head was right, belly was full and now tired of watching *Martin* re-runs, I went and climbed in bed with Juanita. She im-mediately fitted herself to me, like two spoons in a drawer.

"You hungry?" she asked, half-awake. Always trying to feed me.

"Naw. I warmed up those lamb chops you grilled the other day."

"I'm sorry, honey," said Juanita. "I should've asked if you were hungry before I laid my tired butt down. I'll cook you a special meal tonight, to make it up to you. Okay?"

I told her she could feed me a special meal right now.

"You're so bad!" Juanita said. But she fed me the special meal I'd asked for anyway.

Months after reaching Las Vegas and settling down with Juanita in our tract house, complete with all types of televisions and computer games to combat the monotony of forced reclusiveness, I began to slowly adjust to my new life. Juanita helped me make the adjustment by being as sweet and accommodating as a nigga could ever expect a shawdy to be. Sometimes I'd be in one of my moods when I didn't wanna talk, hug or kiss, nothing but blaze a joint and get lost in my thoughts. Replaying the past in my head.

I'd think about my sister more than anything. My choices had cost Toi her life! If I had known where Rich Kid was, I would've gone back to the ATL to serve him the same ill fate he'd served my peeps. I missed her like crazy! I kept a picture of her in my backpack. I planned to get her name tatted on my shoulder one day.

Also, I hated that Kyree got scratched out before he really had a chance to make up for lost time in the pen, but he had understood that each and every time a nigga picked up that steel and went to take what he wanted, there was a chance he wouldn't walk out of there. That was as much a part of the jack game as taking a nigga's cheddar. His death was ill, but I could swallow it.

Pete, on the other hand, I smiled whenever I remembered blasting that fool. How he thought he could turn his back on me, with a banger in my hand, was unexplainable.

I was blazing a joint, wondering if Keisha had shit in ATL on lock when my eyes damn near bucked out of my skull.

"Oh, shit!"

On the television screen were mug shots of me, Lonnie and Delina, starring on tonight's episode of *America's Most Wanted*. The show depicted all three of us as ruthless killers, me as a monster. I didn't like it when the host of the show called us *cowards*.

How a nigga gon' be a ruthless killer, a monster *and* a coward? They labeled a nigga a mass murderer and a psychopath, too. Said police suspected me of other murders besides the ones in Lithonia, Georgia.

Ain't that some shit?

For the next two weeks, I didn't leave the house at all. I watched the street from the front window, both burners in hand.

Juanita asked if I would feel more at ease if we went to stay at a hotel for a while. At that particular time, I wasn't leaving the door unless it was in a body bag. Otherwise, I was staying out of sight.

What I really needed was some real artillery. Some assault rifles and body armor, so whenever po-po did come my way, they mamas could get out their black dresses.

The Las Vegas paper advertised gun shows and conventions all of the time. Maybe I would venture out of the crib and check one out.

My only concern, then, was that cops probably went to those gun shows, too, trying to see what was the latest shit on the market for bad guys. And I had too much respect for Juanita to send her on a mission like that.

Weeks passed with no bum-rush from the FBI, and I began to relax a little. To be on the safe side, we moved to another place about twenty minutes away. Breaking leases were costly, but money wasn't a thang.

Again we found a crib on a nice, quiet street, though not on a cul-de-sac this time. This crib had four bedrooms, two and a half baths and a den to go along with the average-size living and dining rooms and a good size kitchen.

I had one of the bedrooms soundproofed and turned into a small recording studio, complete with an electronic beat machine, sampler and other equipment needed to record quality tracks.

I spent mad hours in my recording studio making wack shit, at first, but then I got kinda dope the more time I spent polishing my skills and getting better at mixing beats and sampling music.

It was really just something to combat the boredom while Juanita was at class or gone to build with her people.

Inside the studio room, I put on the headphones and turned on the dope tracks I had laid the other day. Satisfied with the track, I sat down and wrote the lyrics:

It's the g-h-e-t-t-o that's got a nigga 'bout to scream/Fuck dat/I'm chasin' my dreams, my nigga/ by any means/Or could it be meant for me to struggle/ass out in the streets looking for a hustle/while fake rappers go from petty crime to stolen cars/to slangin' dub sacks/ to crack supastars/all in one bar/that shit ain't trill on the boulevards/where every day ghetto drama got a nigga high on weed/cocking that Smith & Wesson/ready to go take what I need/don't call it greed/'cause I'm trying to rule the hood/why da fuck should I struggle while others livin' hella good?/street mafuckaz know I flow true/like toes on one foot/we all in the same shoe/caught up in the same ghetto game/murking mafuckaz 'cause they violate our name/or 'cause our stash don't weigh the same/from year to year don't shit change/so who's to blame for the infinite pain?/You can't blame us/we didn't bring ourselves here in chains.

Completing the first verse, I put the pen down and practiced rapping the lyrics over the beats, over and over until my delivery was tight, then I wrote the hook and the rest of the song.

By the time I finished, three hours later, the shit was phat! I titled it *Ghetto Drama: Don't blame us!* Then I listened to the finished version over and over, pretending that it wasn't my own joint, asking myself would I bump it in my whip if some other nigga had made it. Maybe it was hard for me to judge my own shit, but the shit still sounded phat to me.

Juanita was through studying her lessons when I came out of the studio room to get her so she could listen to my joint.

She wasn't a fan of gangsta rap but she was from the hood and still knew what was dope and what was wack. Besides, it wasn't like Juanita was a religious fanatic or up on a high horse, despising hip-hop.

She had to love hip hop 'cause she loved me and I personified the game. Plus, rap and hip-hop was just an expression of our culture and she was down with that, fo'sho'.

She appreciated the stories told through gangsta lyrics, she just didn't choose to purchase those artist's joints. It wasn't like shawdy plugged her ears when I bumped certain rapper's shit.

Besides, I gave Juanita mad props for walking the talk. She claimed to love her black people and our culture, and she backed her claims up with action. She shopped at black-owned stores, tutored young black kids in a program at the university, watched black television shows, read mad biographies and autobiographies about blacks, the whole nine.

She was in the kitchen fixing dinner when I stepped to her.

"Yo. I want you to check out something and tell me if you like it," I interrupted Juanita's dinner preparations.

"Okay. Let me turn the oven down some." I smelled the aroma of homemade turkey pot pies wafting from the oven when she opened the oven door to check them and adjust the heat.

Juanita bobbed her head and tapped her foot to the beat coming out of the headphones, as she listened to *Ghetto Drama*.

"Play it back," she said after it had gone off.

She had me play the song for her three times before she took the headphones off.

"Boo," she said, "that's real good!"

"You like it for real?"

"For real!" Juanita maintained.

"Even though it's gangsta?" I asked.

"Yeah. And even though the lyrics are gansta, there's still social consciousness in your message. Especially the hook, and in the third verse. Plus the beat is really good!" Juanita commented, giving me props.

I told her she would give me props even if the shit was wack. I was her nigga.

"But I wouldn't lie to you," she said. "I don't think you'd want me to do that. You've got skills. I'm not gassing you up."

I laughed. "What you know about skillz and gassin somebody up? You spittin' slang now, huh?" I said, cracking up.

"Hey," Juanita said, hands on hips, bobbing her neck like hood girls do. "I'm from the projects, too."

Shawdy couldn't have been gassin' a nigga up 'cause some days she'd taken the song with her and listened to it in the car on her way to and from school.

Feeling good about Ghetto Drama, I decided to do a whole CD.

Time passed, and with it came good news. Juanita was carrying my seed. That really wasn't a huge surprise since she didn't use contraceptives, nor did we use protection when we made love. And, of course, I've always been a potent nigga. So we both knew that it was just a matter of time before she conceived my seed.

I had kept it real with her, reminding her that life together could never be normal. Nor could I promise that I wouldn't have to jet away without her and my seed, never seeing them again if my past started closing in on me. I questioned if I was interfering with Juanita's goals or possibly strapping too much weight on her back if I had to bounce and left her with a child to raise without a father.

"No, baby," said Juanita. "Nothing short of death will stop me from completing my studies and reaching my professional goals. If the worst happens and we have to be without you, know that I'm going to raise a strong black man, a god. Or a strong queen if it's a girl. And it'll be your blood in our child's veins, nothing can ever change that."

"True. And I believe you'll hold it down if I ever have to bounce," I said.

"You know I will, baby."

I reached and hugged her. "I wish I could take you out somewhere to celebrate. I know you gotta hate living like this. I can't go nowhere with you and shit."

"No, baby. I could never hate anything concerning us. True, at times I wish it wasn't this way 'cause I'd be proud to go in public on your arm.

However, I understood the situation before today. You were up front with me from the start. I chose to get involved with you anyway, and I haven't regretted it so far."

Since I couldn't take Juanita out to dinner to celebrate, I surprised her with a candlelight dinner that weekend.

I used the Yellow Pages to call around until I found a catering company that could hook me up a special meal. From over the phone, the caterer described several dishes that they could prepare. I chose the grilled wild duck marinated in lemon-mustard and honey sauce, served with wild rice, stuffed grilled tomatoes, wild green beans, and a fresh baked whole loaf of bread.

That was the main course, the entrée. The appetizer would be broiled lobster tail, shrimp cocktails and a three-cheese salad. Dessert was chilled cinnamon apricot hearts.

The caterer offered to send a server along to set up table decorations and to serve. I told the person on the phone that I'd handle the decorations and serving myself as long as they sent all of the necessary utensils and stuff.

Like I've always maintained, everyone had a routine, so I knew that once Juanita left the house Saturday evening, she wouldn't be back until nine or nine-fifteen. She would be bringing home fish dinners from a seafood place not too far from where we lived. That was her Saturday routine. Only I would surprise her this Saturday.

A few minutes after nine, I heard the Cressida pull into the driveway next to the Ford Explorer. A few minutes later, I met Juanita at the front door and took the styro-foam trays from her. True to form they were fish dinners.

"You must be starving," Juanita said after greeting me with the customary kiss. "I'm hungry, too. Let me have those back, I'll put the food on real plates."

"No, boo." I stopped her from heading to the kitchen. "You go get dressed as if we were going out to dinner. I have a little surprise for you."

"What? You want me to take a shower and get dressed up?"

164

"Yep, but be quick."

While Juanita used the shower in the master bedroom to get ready, I used one of the others to do the same. Needless to say, I was showered and dressed a half-hour before Juanita. Of course, all I had to do after getting out the shower was lotion down, splash on some cologne and put on the silk Coogi pajama set Juanita had bought for me months ago.

I put Jaheim's CD on and the music played at a soft volume throughout the house. Once the candles were lit, all I had to do was wait for my beautiful shawdy to appear.

She came out the bedroom in an earth colored silk wrap-around dress that flowed down to the floor with a matching head wrap—an Egyptian Queen. Wood bangles on her wrists. The diamond inter-locking hearts pin, pinned above her heart.

I put my elbow out for her hand and led her into the dining room.

Two twin sets of candles burned in holders on the table. I pulled out a chair for her and then handed her a long-stemmed rose that I had in a vase near the china cabinet.

Jaheim set the mood while I served the appetizer. The main course remained heated in aluminum serving trays with little fire canisters that burned under them, supplied by the caterer.

After the appetizer, I used the CD remote to change Jaheim to Lyfe while I served the main course along with the Asti Spumante for myself. Juanita didn't drink alcoholic beverages, so I had ordered some type of fruit-flavored water that came in an elegant bottle for her. We both were too stuffed to do anything more than taste the dessert afterwards.

Shawdy thanked me for the dinner, then she got up and began removing our dishes from the table.

I stopped her. "Sit down, boo. It's all on me tonight."

Juanita smiled as she watched me clean the dishes from the table, put the leftover food in Tupperware and into the freezer. She knew it wasn't my steelo to do anything domestic, and I think she appreciated that I'd did it for her.

When I was done, I joined Juanita in the living room on the couch, clicked Lyfe to Carlos Santana, one of Juanita's favorite jazz artists.

After the food had settled and the jazz music worked us into an even more relaxed mood, we slow danced, record after record. It wasn't that I had turned into a romantic-ass nigga. I was still a G at heart. I was just trying to do something special for my shawdy, to let her know that she was appreciated.

My surprise romantic evening must've had an effect on Juanita because that night she was all over me in bed, and being the aggressor wasn't her style. I wasn't complaining, though.

"Do that thang, girl," I teased when she straddled me.

"You so bad," she blushed.

CHAPTER 20

"Hello," Inez said after taking my call from a coworker that had told her I was on line three, "this is Miss Patterson."

"Miss Patterson, this is the gentleman that services your car. How are you today?"

"I'm fine, thank you. And yourself?"

"Fine. How's your car holding up?"

"Very well. It's no longer running hot."

"Good," I said. "Listen, can you drop off my tools at your mother's house when you get off work today?"

"Huh? Oh—oh—yeah—yes, I can. I'm sorry for not leaving them in my garage," Inez recovered and followed my code-talk. "Would you like me to drop them off on my lunch break?"

"No. After work will be fine."

"Okay."

"Goodbye."

I didn't know if Inez exactly understood my message but a few minutes past six o'clock that evening she came pouncing through her Ma Dukes door.

"Mama! Has anyone called for me yet?"

Then she saw me in the living room, lights out, curtains drawn closed, holding Tamia. She squealed and then caught herself. In an instant, she was showering my face with kisses.

"Oh, my God! I thought I would never see you again," cried Inez.

"You know I wasn't gonna let that happen. Stop crying and give me a taste of those lips." I covered her mouth with mine and we kissed for an eternity.

When our lips finally parted Inez was out of breath. "I missed you so much," she managed to breathe out.

"I know, shawdy. I missed you, too." I hugged her tighter.

167

Inez' mother left out of the room to allow us some privacy. We set on the sofa and talked for hours, holding hands the entire time.

I stayed until it was dark out, then I kissed Inez and Tamia goodbye, put on my overcoat and my disguise, fake beard and eye patch, checked my gats and slipped away the same route I had used to slip in.

Keisha picked me up from Ma Duke's crib in her brand new Humvee.

"What's up, shawdy?" I slid in the passenger seat.

"You! Damn, nigga, it's good to see you!" she beamed.

When we got down the street, she pulled over to the curb and parked. I reached at my waist for my burner.

I know this ho ain't 'bout to cross me!

She peeped my reaction.

"Nigga, it ain't even like that. I'd die before I would sell you out. You don't know?"

"What the fuck you park for?"

"So you can give me a hug. I didn't wanna ask for one back there. I figured your girl might be peeking out the window," explained Keisha. "Now quit trippin' and give a bitch a hug."

After we hugged, Keisha said, "Dayum, I wanna fuck you," pulling off from the curb.

"Ain't Angel keepin' you happy?" I teased.

"What? That bitch is too through."

"Say what?"

"Yep. I don't fuck around like that no more. Shit had got crazy. She had gotten so possessive I could hardly breathe! I had to bust a cap in her, just to get away from her *Fatal Attraction* ass!"

"You shot her?" I asked in disbelief.

"Yep. Butsted that hoe in the arm for tryna *strong-arm* a bitch, and in the leg for always *kickin'* that stupid shit."

I laughed like hell. "So what's up? You through fuckin' with chicks?"

"Yeah, that shit was just a phase with me. I got a big-head college boy that I'm fuckin' with."

"A college boy? I thought you liked thugs?"

"I do, but until I meet one as thorough as you, I'm not interested."

"Yeah, yeah. Anyway, you raping the game or what?"

"Got it in a chokehold."

As we drove on, Keisha explained how she was puttin' it down but then we began discussing my true reasons for returning to the ATL.

Rich Kid had resurfaced.

Keisha had informed me of his reappearance through Inez.

She had copped a four-bedroom ranch-style crib out in Fayetteville to get away from wolves that were privy to her come up and were salivating at a chance to jack her.

"I see you're living real good," I complimented.

"Yeah, I flipped the dope you left with me. Now I have a regular connect."

"Who?"

"You don't know them. But Rich Kid stepped to me a few months ago about shopping with him," she said as we went inside her crib and sat down in the living room.

"Don't he know you used to fuck with me?"

"Naw. Remember, he was off the scene when you were frontin' me work. And nobody knows you left me all that shit. Niggaz still tryna figure out how I came up so lovely. Rich Kid asked the same thing. I told him loose lips lead to indictments.

"Anyway, he's just gettin' back out there like that, so he needs somebody to shop with him 'cause most of his old customers got new connects while he was out of the game. Plus, I heard some of his people hit him for an ass of dope while he was laid up. You know how the streets talk."

I nodded, indicating that I knew exactly where she was coming from.

"Anyway, as soon as the nigga stepped to me I started rockin' his ass to sleep, waiting for you to get at Inez so we could let you know the business. I done fucked and sucked the nigga, keepin' him close until I could deliver him to you."

"That's what's up," I said. "But the Rich Kid I knew ain't nobody's fool. You can't just call him up and tell him to come to your spot? And if he does come, won't he be rollin' with his goons?"

"Naw, baby, ever since you tried to get at him and then his people crossed him, that nigga don't fuck with dudes like that. Really, I think he done fell off some 'cause he straight roll dolo."

"Nah, that nigga ain't hurtin', he paid. He just livin' by the code: *Trust No Man*. But fuck all that, how you gon' deliver that nigga to me?"

"On a silver platter, baby boy."

"I'ma love that."

"I know. It'll be my way of thanking you for trusting a bitch. That was a lot of work you left me with. And for real, I didn't even know I could handle it," she admitted.

"I knew you could. Now gon' make that call, but don't press him. Trust, he ain't stupid."

"Man, relax, I got this", she said, picking up her cordless house phone.

I listened on a second cordless phone that Keisha handed me from off of the end table next to the couch we sat on, as she talked to Rich Kid.

"We might be able to do some business but we need to talk numbers," Keisha said after Rich Kid brought up the subject.

"Not over the phone," he cautioned.

"Okay, get at me when you wanna talk. But make it soon, I gotta eat," she replied.

"I'ma holla," he said before hanging up.

He seemed to be taking the bait.

Since I expected to have to stay in ATL a few days, I sent Keisha to go scoop Inez. I knew that the Feds could easily be watching her, but I just took a chance, figuring ain't no way in fuck they could watch her 24/7. I had been a fugitive for over a year.

Inez and I spent a passionate night together in one of Keisha's guest rooms.

In the morning, we said a heart-wrenching goodbye, then Keisha dropped Inez back off at home.

Later, around seven-thirty that evening, Rich Kid pulled into Keisha's driveway unannounced.

Dolo.

I listened from the adjoining room, crouched down behind a bookcase. Keisha let Rich Kid in and offered him a seat in the living room.

"Would you like a drink or something?" she asked.

"Nah, I'm short on time. Let's talk business. How much work you tryna fuck with?" he cut straight to the chase.

"That depends on the price," she responded.

They were saying some other shit, but I didn't really hear them. The fury inside of me had muted the conversation. All I heard was Rich Kid's voice echoing, *Bitch nigga, you missed! I didn't.*

That punk mafucka had my precious sister murdered and had called me up to boast about it! Tauntin' me like I was too small of a nigga to get at his ass.

Now, nigga, what? Even the strong and mighty can get caught slippin'.

"Well, the price is negotiable," he was saying to Keisha.

"But your life ain't, nigga!" I replied, stepping into the living room, a burner in each had, locked and loaded.

Rich Kid's head snapped around toward my voice as he jumped up from the couch, ready to take flight. When he saw my face he seemed to shrink, and a whine escaped from his mouth like a bitch.

This hoe ass nigga definitely didn't pull the trigger. He had someone else kill my fam, just like he used to pay me to murk niggas. He ain't no killa, he's a bitch. A bitch with dough.

"Man up, punk!" I spat as I moved in just a few feet away from him, both burners ready to go the fuck off.

Keisha stood up from the sofa, sliding a .380 from under the cushion. She pointed it at Rich Kid's chest.

"His enemies are my enemies," she exclaimed.

I expected him to reach for his waist 'cause he had to know it was a do-or-die situation. But like I'd said time and time again, Rich Kid wasn't a killa. He always paid a mafucka to do his dirty work.

Now that it was time to bust his guns, the nigga smelled like pussy.

"Y'all hold up!" he cried, throwing his hands in the air.

To think I ever respected this bitch!

"Hear me out!" he pleaded.

172

"Toi was my heart, mafucka," I said real calm-like. "Our beef wasn't hers."

"Man, *you* drew first blood! What the fuck I ever do to you to make you gun at me?" he cried.

"Bitch nigga, you ain't in no position to ask me shit! Die wondering!"

Blocka! Blocka!

He reached out for my arm.

Blocka!

When he crumpled to the floor with his melon leaking, Keisha came over and pumped two in his chest.

"Damn, shawdy, when did you get so trill with it?" I asked, looking at her with my mouth hanging open.

"Man, like you, I'm Englewood born and bred."

A minute later, we wrapped Rick Kid's body in bedspreads, loaded him inside of his whip and left that bitch nigga stinkin' on a dark road in College Park.

Rest in peace, Toi, I thought as I slid into the passenger seat of Keisha's whip and left the scene.

Ca$h

CHAPTER 21

I made it back to Nevada with no trouble. Before leaving ATL, I had gone to my money-stash spot and got another backpack full of Benjamins.

My boo was so happy and relieved I made it back, she didn't leave my side at all for a full week. When she did, I jumped back into my studio.

I had compiled four tracks, *Ghetto Drama, Blood & Money, Your Woman, My Bitch!* and *You Live in My Heart*, a tribute to my sister.

Now I was penning a joint for niggaz on lockdown:

It ain't over my niggaz even though it feels that way/ and every night I pray y'all soldiers see a better day/ and for all my road dawgs/ even though I made it home/ I can't leave y'all alone/ so I rep' you in my songs/ and every time I reminisce it gets a nigga teary-eyed/ I know you heard 'bout my peeps, and knew a nigga had to ride/ he fucked with my pride/ so had to come strong/ now he's dead and gone/ no apologies for splittin' his dome/ 'cause I was forced to settle shit with the steel/ being project raised with the will/ that made it easy to kill/ the shit's fa-real when a nigga is broke/ no fly whip, no hos/ no 'dro to smoke/ so who's to blame for these hard ass times?/ my tribulations got me blind/ and I can't find peace of mind/ so I get high to relieve the pain/ and do the crimes/ so when it's my time/ the world gon' remember my name/ y'all niggaz try to maintain/ I'd rather die young than be a pawn in this dirty game/ 'cause in the game, it's staring at the crossroads/ or in a cell serving life, with a lost soul.

2nd Verse

Five long years of blood and tears in them white folks chain gang/ remember how we would wild to keep from going insane?/ Nothin' to lose/ Nothin' to gain/ But the world can't feel our pain/if they ain't never been locked down without a key to remove the chains/ Nigga/ how the fuck you figga that times can't get so hard/ when you a free man/ and my ghetto soldiers are millions locked behind bars/ paying dues for some shit they did that made the news/ suckaz be screamin' soldier/ but they can't rock a soldier's shoes/ if your mic tales were true/ you couldn't wax about what you do/ My nigga/I walk the talk/ I'll body bag your whole crew.

I put the pen down and rapped the lyrics over a beat I already produced.

The first verse flowed phat, but I had to go back and rework part of the second verse and add some bass to it before writing the third verse.

By the time Juanita got home from school and hooked up dinner, I had the fifth track completed, which I titled: *For My Niggaz on Lock.* Then I penned a tribute to Inez over the instrumental of Tupac's *Are You Still Down.*

When I wasn't in my studio and Juanita was away, I spent hours thinking about Inez. Shawdy was too down for me to just forget. I would also think about Keisha. Shawdy was doin' the damn thang! I had sensed her loyalty, but truth be told, I had slept on her gangsta.

My boo was gangsta, too. Just in a different way. One that was elevated beyond the streets. I witnessed that when I accompanied her to a meeting with her people, a month after my return from the A.

The cipher was peace.

I went with Juanita mostly out of curiosity to see what all this Five Percenter, culture, science babble she stressed was all about. There were three other people there besides the four I had met that once: Wisdom Born, Understanding and a female named Destiny, whom I was told was *newborn*.

I had never been a religious person, though if I would've taken time to think about it, I probably believed in God. I told the group I believed in a Supreme Being I just didn't claim any certain religion.

"So," responded Wise Professor, "you believe God is a mysterious spook in the sky? Somewhere up in heaven, looking down over you?"

"Yeah," I said, somewhat defensively.

"Who taught you to believe that?" His tone unchanged.

"My Ma Duke, I guess."

"And who taught *her* to believe that?"

"Probably her Ma Dukes."

He took me back generations until we reached the point where it became obvious that my concept of God and religion was really a concept taught to my ancestors by Europeans and white slave masters from America, who had brainwashed black people around the world.

Wise Professor said, "We are the supreme beings. The Asiatic black man, the original man. We're God. I'm God. You're God."

I must've had a look of disbelief on my face.

He continued, "You're just eighty-five right now. You don't know your true culture. God is the sole controller of the universe, the Supreme being or black man that understands his true culture—Islam."

He explained that Islam meant. I, Self, Lord and Master. And in the case of women, I, Self, Love, Allah's Mathematics. Islam, he said, is for the black men, women and children's true culture. It's their way of life.

I'm not the type of nigga to go for no smoke and mirrors game, no matter what form it comes in, so I was quick to question the claim that any man is God. I could go for the black man being the original man. Shit, somebody had to be here first. And Wise Professor's explanation of how the white man came into existence wasn't impossible to believe.

"I can show and prove that the black man is God," Wise Professor claimed.

"Show and prove," I challenged him.

"No doubt," he replied, and then he proceeded to prove his claim.

I listened attentively, and I had to agree with what he was saying.

At home that night, I continued discussing with Juanita all the things Wise Professor had to say, plus the other things they'd discussed amongst one another. Some of the shit I hadn't understood.

"That's because we were speaking in Supreme Alphabets and Mathematics," explained Juanita.

"I feel you," I said, respecting her thing.

The cipher had been serious. The type of love for the hood and our people they had expressed was different from the type love I had for niggaz and the hood.

My love for the hood meant that no place was better, I liked the shit that went down on the daily and I missed that mafucka when I wasn't whippin' the block.

My love for my niggaz meant I wanted to see 'em get cheddar and shine. Or get married and square-up, if that's what they wanted to do. It meant that I would ride with 'em if they needed a killa for the job. And it meant they were immune from my heater as long as they showed me the same respect.

To Juanita and Wise, having love for their people and the hood meant something much different. It meant educating them, teaching black people their true culture, delivering them from the triple stages of darkness and helping them become clean and purified mentally as well as physically. It meant uplifting black people.

It damn sho' didn't mean the type of love I stressed for the hood. Or maybe it did, just taken to another level.

"What did dude mean when he said I was eighty-five?" I asked Juanita a few days later. "Is it cool for you to explain that?"

"Yeah, I can explain it."

She wrote it down on paper for me:

5 percent –poor, righteous teachers who do not believe in the teachings of the 10 percent. 5 percent who are all wise and know who the true living god is. He teaches that the true living god is the Son of Man, the Supreme Being, the black man from Asia who teaches freedom, justice and equality to all human families of the earth. Otherwise known as civilized people, and also Muslim and Muslim sons and daughters.

10 percent: the rich, the slave makers of the poor, who teach the poor lies to believe that the Almighty, and true living god, is a spook that cannot be seen with the naked eye. Otherwise known as the blood suckers of the poor.

85 percent: the uncivilized people, poisonous animal eaters, slave of the mental death and power. People who do not know their own origin. Those who worship what they know not, who are easily led in the wrong direction, but hard to be led in the right direction.

As soon as I finished reading what Juanita had written, I was thinking, *How dude gon' call me uncivilized? Nobody had led me in the wrong direction.*

"I chose my own course in life," I told Juanita.

179

Ca$h

"Not really, boo," she said. "See, by the time you chose what direction to go in, the powers that already conspired to make you feel that *that* was your only way out of the hood. So, in essence, you *were* led in the wrong direction."

I got mad as hell. How my shawdy gon' say some ill shit like dat? Like I had been a sheep, being led to slaughter. Crackers hadn't made me do shit. Wasn't any white folks in my hood.

I went in to my studio room and penned the final track on Side-A of my demo. I titled it Young Gun:

This is my story not a song/ my name is Youngblood/ it should be Young Gun/ while y'all was out rockin' a party/ I was clockin' my first body/ whip fast/ ski mask/ clip blast/ dipped with the cash/ rolled a blunt/ got high and drunk/ went deep up in your girl's ass/ not yours, his/ the nigga at home with the kids/ while she was with the young one/ Youngblood, the Young Gun/ call it my story, not a song.

I completed the lyrics then tested them over different beats until I found a track that worked. My studio room had become not only a sanctuary against boredom, but it was also an outlet for my rage.

Juanita's people, Wise Professor and 'em, was sleepin' on me if they considered me eighty-five! Murder Mike had probably thought the same shit!

As the months passed by and Juanita's belly grew large with my seed, I had come to embrace the teaching of Five Percenters. Which was only the teaching of truth, of knowledge and of self. Knowledge of one's origin and true culture. Enlightenment. All of which opened my eyes to things that I'd been blind to, or not exposed to, before now.

I came to understand how certain things that were perpetrated against blacks in America generations ago, continued to affect the present generation. And though I still felt that on a conscious level my choices had been my own, I understood the dynamics that influenced my decisions and what had been important to me: the fly gear, the bling, the street fame, respect, even my blatant disregard for my life and the enemies I targeted. On the other hand, being a thugged-out nigga was part of who I was. I had regrets, but no apologies.

The further along I got in my studies, the more knowledge I gained. I became aware that although I had always been a good father to my seeds, I had contributed to the decimation of the black family by not creating a true and strong family structure.

The one thing I had trouble with was seeing *all* black women as queens. I had seen too many shawdies that were flat-out bitches and hoes!

But the science behind that was that those shawdies were going against their true nature and weren't conscious of their true worth. Just as many dudes were not conscious of who *they* were.

Now that I had progressed beyond the Supreme Mathematics, Alphabets, Student Enrollment and lessons one through thirty-six, I could relate to the science certain rappers, like Wu Tang Clan, Nas, and Mob Deep were spittin' on wax.

Before I had knowledge of self and became God Body, I would listen to those artists but not really understand the science in their lyrics.

Also, I remember trippin' when I read that Andre 3000 and Erykah Badu had named their son Seven, a number. Of course, I was eighty-five back then, and the science was beyond my comprehension. I knew now that the number seven was God in the Supreme Mathematics, and the 7th letter in the Supreme Alphabet was God.

As my knowledge grew, I would build when we held a cipher and Juanita and I would build together at the crib. The science brought us together even closer than before. She was my earth and I was her sun. Our child would be our star.

When I saw the eight-point star daggling from the necklace around Juanita's neck now, I knew what it represented. *The black family.*

Juanita gave birth to our star, a seven-and-a-half-pound boy whom we named Justice Lord McPherson, giving him her last name because I could not take a chance and sign the birth certificate. So in the place on the birth certificate for father's name, Juanita wrote my attribute: Young Lord Magnetic.

I regretted that I wasn't able to be in the delivery room with Juanita when Justice came into the world, but my Earth understood. However, I was able to welcome them home a couple days later.

My son was paper sack brown, a combination of me and Juanita's complexions. Otherwise, he was all me.

With the strength shown by generations of black women, Juanita was up and about, back in class, being a mother and wifey and taking care of the house soon after coming home from the hospital.

I still spent hours in my studio room working on the B-side of the demo I was making. The B-side would reflect my evolution. Knowledge was wasted if it was not used or shared to enlighten and uplift my black people.

I wrote:

Imagine a time/ when all black people shine/ when the biggest crime is being culturally blind/ a hood where all our kids grow up the right way/ imagine it, gods/ it's a fantasy, the blind say/ a whole generation/ receiving proper education/ no more petty crimes/ now we're legal paper chasin'/ No more tax evasion/ no more charges to be facin'/ no more mental sedation/ or crack heads basin'/ we got doctors and lawyers/ architects and engineers/ investment brokers/ CEOs and women peers/ we can unite and fight/ take the hood to new heights/ have mad peaceful nights/ much more than civil rights/ I love being black/ to all my thugs and college cats/ still spittin' ammo at your dome/ but not the kind that come from gats...

Juanita helped write the hook and the rest of the track and she titled it *Evolution*.

She couldn't rap a lick, but she wrote hella poetry, which was the cousin of rap. In fact, I planned to use a poem she wrote titled *Gods of the Earth* as the Outro when I completed side B.

By the time I finished the whole CD, Justice was almost four-months old. I was still laying low, used to not going out of the house much by now.

I'd remained in touch with Inez and with Lonnie through her. My dawg was maintaining, him and his family were safe and laying low somewhere. Inez, Tamia and Bianca were at peace. I was always glad to know that. Inez was being a soldier, maintaining love for me, but I wasn't gonna sell her no empty box of dreams. She deserved more respect than that. Which was why I told her to go on with her life, find a man who would love her, the kids and treat 'em all with the utmost.

I verbalized to her, for the first time, what she had to have already concluded: *there was no way we'd ever be able to be together again. My legal problems prohibited me from ever returning to the ATL or living a normal life. It also wouldn't be wise for Inez to try to come to me.*

"I'll always care for you," I told her.

She cried, of course. It was hard to tell her that I had a four-month-old son and someone I loved, but I told her as gently as was possible over the phone. I made it clear that my new family had nothing to do with us not having a future together.

"My problems with the law won't allow it."
Inez knew that was the truth.
"Is it Juanita?" she asked, though I hadn't given her the slightest hint.
I couldn't lie to her. She'd been too real with me.
"Yeah."
"I figured you were with her," she said with pain in her voice.
I didn't want her to say goodbye like that, for several reasons. Most of all, I truly did care about her. We'd rode down and dirty together, Bonnie and Clyde-style. It was important to me, for her to know that I had mad love and respect for her and circumstances, more than anything, had torn us apart. I promised her that I wouldn't forget her and Tamia and as long as I breathed, she'd hear from me. There was still pain in her voice when we said goodbye, but I felt she had appreciated my honesty.

I considered Juanita my wife even though we hadn't walked down the aisle. Our vows were to each other, and we didn't need a paper document to quantify what we meant to one another. The harmony between us was incredible, like we were of one mind.

If the hood could see me now!

But my evolution did not make me weak or hen-pecked. It simply allowed me to appreciate my beautiful, strong Earth, my black woman.

Juanita submitted to me because that was her rightful role, one that she embraced because she knew that it was right and exact. I was the sun. She was the moon and received her light from me, which reflected to the star, Justice Lord, our son.

CHAPTER 22

I was lying on the couch in the living room, with Justice climbing all over me while Juanita read aloud the thesis she had written for one of her classes. She was a few months away from earning her B.S. before she'd go on to medical school.

"So, what do you think of it?" asked Juanita.

"It's good," I said.

"Did you understand the basis of it?"

"No doubt. I'm not as intelligent as you are, but I comprehend," I offered.

"Intelligence comes in many forms." It was one of her favorite sayings.

"Come to Mommy, Justice. Let daddy relax."

Justice wasn't hearing that, though. He was spoiled, but not rotten. However, he was always up under me since I was home with him all day while Juanita was in class or doing intern work at the hospital.

Today was a rare day when she got to chill at home with us, maybe study a little.

Later, some Gods were coming by for a cipher. We'd been holding monthly cipher at our crib.

"Come to Mommy, Justice." He shook his head *no*.

I laughed. "He doesn't—"

Boom! Boom! Boom!

The front door came crashing in.

"Don't move, motherfucker!"

"Let me see your hands! Get 'em up! Now! I'll blow your ass away!"

Juanita screamed.

Then she was thrown to the floor with a gun pointed down at her.

My son was crying. Scared.

"Get that fucking gun out of my girl's face!" I screamed.

"Shut up! Hands in the air! Now!"

I followed their instructions but then I thought about the two burners stashed under the couch cushion beneath me. My hand was itching to reach for my heaters.

Fuck going to prison!

But I didn't want my son to get shot. I had promised myself when this day came I was going out, guns blazing, but the mafuckaz had caught me in a situation where I couldn't buck, not without getting Justice and Juanita killed.

They pushed my son off of my chest, pushed me to the floor, mashing my face in the carpet, handcuffed me and kicked me in the face.

They started reading me my rights. "You're under arrest for murder, armed robbery and unlawful flight to avoid persecution! You have the right to remain silent, anything..."

"Don't put them handcuffs on her!" I spat, ignoring the pig who was cuffin' me.

Why the fuck were they cuffin' Juanita?

"Ma'am. You're under arrest for harboring a fugitive," a cop was saying.

"Sarge, I found two weapons. We'll charge 'em both for these two beauties."

"Where are you taking my baby?" Juanita cried when she saw Justice being taken out of the front door.

"The child will be in the custody of Family and Children Services."

"Lieutenant, there's a street full of television cameras outside."

"Well, he is a mass murderer. Enjoy your fifteen minutes of fame."

Juanita was crying and begging the cops to let her take Justice with her. She questioned why did they have to handle me so rough?

Justice was wailing at the top of his lungs, frightened by all the commotion. I was concerned for my family, but I was stoic in the face of the cameras. If the world was watching, they weren't gonna see me acting punked out.

My situation was grave, no doubt, but what could I do now? The bastards had me cuffed and surrounded by dozens of FBI agents and local police.

Just as I was being pushed into the back of an unmarked police car, I saw Wise Professor and the other Gods in our cipher trying to push their way past police and the throng of news people.

I had two immediate thoughts: One, I'd never be free again. Two, *Inez!* It had to be her that dropped a dime on me. *Bitches!*

I was extradited to DeKalb County Jail and kept under maximum security.

A month later, Juanita was out on bond, and received permission from a Las Vegas judge to come to Atlanta and assist me in hiring an attorney. She had to use the money from her personal savings account because the FBI had confiscated and filed a seizure claim on the loot I had at the crib when they busted in and arrested us.

I was pissed that those mafuckaz got my loot and had the audacity to wanna keep it! On what grounds? How could they prove the money was obtained illegally?

The prominent attorney hired to represent me explained that, if nothing else, the government would seize the money on tax evasion charges. A'ight. They were playing like dat, huh? I determined right then that they would never get their hands on the rest of my stash.

I was hot about that, but my anger was elevated to an all-time high when I learned from my attorney how the FBI had tracked me down.

Inez hadn't been the guilty rat. Nor had it been one of the Gods in our cipher, as I had sort of thought. Instead, the rat mafucka who'd tipped them off to my whereabouts was the one person I trusted most with my life.

Lonnie!

"You're a goddamn lie!" I'd spat at my attorney when he told me my dawg, my tight man, had snitched me out. But it was true.

Turns out that Lonnie and Delina had got popped in Long Island, New York by undercover DEA agents they had sold ten kilos to.

After they were arrested and their fingerprints were put into the national data base, the DEA agents realized who they had in custody. Two of the three fugitives most wanted for the mass murder in Georgia.

The FBI had kept Lonnie and Delina's capture from the media, hoping to pressure Lonnie into leading them to me. In exchange for the government promising Delina leniency and not seeking the death penalty against him, Lonnie had told them I was with Juanita. They'd tracked us down through her school records and her utility bills.

Lonnie also agreed to testify that I had planned the Lithonia robbery and murders. If that didn't make him a big enough rat, Lonnie agreed to testify about any and all crimes we'd committed together. *And* he told them about me and Inez robbing and murking King in Kentucky.

The Rat Bastard! He had sunk to the lowest form of life—a snitch!

I found out that Lonnie was being housed in Dekalb County Jail, too.

The bitch ass nigga was in protective custody in a cellblock on a different floor from where I was being kept. Through a guard, he sent me a jive saying that he hadn't wanted to snitch me out, but the feds had his nuts in a vise-grip. He and Delina's blood had been found inside the house in Lithonia, and they'd had one of the weapons used in the murders with them the day they'd been busted by the undercover DEA agents.

The rat mafucka claimed he could've taken his medicine like a man, but it was his love and concern for Delina that had made him turn me in.

What about your love and concern for your dawg? Huh? I wrote him back. *And why did he have to drop a dime on Inez?*

The answer to that became evident.

My attorney said Lonnie was giving them the goods, trying to get Delina the best deal he could. So, fuck me and mine, huh?

After Inez was arrested, we were both extradited to Kentucky and charged with murder. The strongest evidence they had against her was hair samples found on the bed sheets where King had been killed and a fingerprint in the bathroom.

Damn!

We had forgotten the sheets that night! Also, the teeth marks on King's arm would match Inez'. The only evidence that could incriminate me of King's murder, unless Inez flipped, was Lonnie's testimony.

His bitch ass was singing like a fuckin' canary!

In Kentucky, Inez' bond was set at three hundred grand. I was, of course, denied bond due to the multiple murder charges I was facing back in ATL.

Keisha came through for Inez, putting up ten percent of the three hundred grand with a bondsman. So, shawdy was released while I was returned to Georgia, back to Dekalb County Jail to await the inevitable.

One day, the guards took me to the yard, inside a fenced in cubicle, and I walked right past Lonnie, who was inside a separate one. He had the nerve to not only look at me, but to say, "It's every man for himself, dawg."

I spat in his face when the guards had to walk him past my cubicle to take him off the yard.

"Bitch ass nigga! I shoulda slumped you, too!" I hurled at his back before getting pulled away by the guards.

CHAPTER 23

The DA decided to seek the death penalty against me in Dekalb County. I wasn't trippin' that shit. In fact, I told Juanita that if I was found guilty, I'd rather get the needle than a sentence of life with no parole, which was a *slow* death. Like DMX said, either let me fly or give me death.

I was housed alone in a cell on the eighth floor of the jail. This was protocol for inmates in my predicament. The solitude allowed me to think over all of my mistakes. I hadn't made many, but the ones I made were huge. Murder Mike had always tried to tell me that Lonnie was flawed. I just couldn't peep it, though.

Still, I shoulda adhered to the code of the streets: *Trust No Man.*

Every time I thought about Lonnie's betrayal, that shit twisted my face! A guard named Lumpkin approached my cell. He'd come to take me to my visit.

"You ready?" asked Lumpkin, peeking through the small rectangular window in the center of the metal cell door.

"Yeah."

He unlocked the tray flap and I stuck my hands through the hole to cuff up. Lumpkin pretended to be cool and maybe he really was, but he still wore a badge, so I never had much to say to him. I assumed he was tryna play me into telling him something he could later use against me in court.

"How you doin' today, dawg?" he asked as he escorted me to my visit.

"I ain't *ya dawg.* But I'm a'ight," I replied.

In visitation, I sat on an iron stool that was bolted to the wall in a small cubicle. Juanita was on the other side of the wire-mesh Plexiglas. We both picked up the phones through which we'd have to converse.

"Peace, God," she said, placing her palm against the Plexi-glas.

"Peace, black woman," I replied, placing my palm against the Plexiglas, too.

"How's my seed?"

"He's fine, getting bigger by the day."

"What about you? How you be, baby girl?"

Juanita got teary-eyed.

"I can't believe those devils are going to seek the death penalty against you!" she said bitterly.

"Why not? You know how those crackers get down."

"Still, boo," she replied.

"Don't sweat that shit, Queen. They can't kill *me*. They can only kill my body. But I'll live on through you, Inez, Ma Duke, my seeds and everything in existence. You know the science. They can do what the fuck they want to, but they can those crackers kill your love for me?"

"Never, baby," she vowed with tears falling.

"Can they erase my whole bloodline by puttin' me to sleep?"

"No, they can't."

"A'ight then. Dry those tears, girl. I'm at peace, however it goes."

Juanita wiped her eyes. "Okay, my king. I'll see you

My upcoming trial was receiving a lot of press coverage and was scheduled to be broadcasted on *Court TV*.

Somehow, the media had gotten a hold of the CD's I'd made in my home studio. They played excerpts from certain tracks every time they reported on my upcoming trail, particularly the lyrics from *Young Gun* where I spat, *"While y'all was out rockin' a party/ I was clockin' my first body."*

They also played lyrics from the B-side of the CD, which I recorded after my evolution to God body.

Pay attention while I spit on the level/Expose you to the devil/The white man/ That's his hand on that Glock/His dope on your block/His conspiracy that killed Pac/His fake religion that ya mama taught you/Check the name on the gear your shawdy bought you/It ain't made by us/In whose God should we trust/A spook in the sky/Or the gods that can be seen with the naked eye/ Fuck beefin' over turf/We control the whole universe/Black man, do the knowledge so you'll overstand the devil's plan.

The news media used my lyrics to paint a picture of a young remorseless killer, a racist and atheist.

Whatever. The CD, of which I'd dubbed several copies, was a hot commodity. With the help of Keisha and Swag, the up-North dude whom I had cut up in a battle rap in Englewood, they took the CD underground and it blew up.

Swag had just signed with a major label, and I had recorded a coupla verses for his CD over the phone in jail. The streets were anxious for Swag's joint to drop.

After several months of wrestling with Dekalb County Jail officials, my attorney was able to get a court order that allowed Inez to visit me. Since she was my co-defendant on the case in Kentucky, jail officials had been denying her visitation requests. But my attorney had successfully argued in court, that because she was the mother of my child, she had the right to see me.

Now, as I looked at Inez through the Plexiglas, my heart went out to her. She was a true thoroughbred.

Her hair was in a long bob, her nails were done and her neck and wrist were frozen. Shawdy looked so damn jazzy and fine. If she was stressing over the murder charge in Kentucky, it didn't show on her face.

"Hey, playgirl," I said into the phone. "You lookin' like you belong in *Black Tail.*"

"Thanks." She stood up and turned around so that I could get a good view of her Apple Bottom.

"I wish I could hit that right about now."

"Me too," she smiled, sitting back down.

Although we spoke on the phone every day, I still asked how she was doing.

I'm straight," she said.

"Check it, shawdy. I've been thinkin'. With Lonnie's and his rat bitch's testimony, these crackers gon' convict me here in Georgia. You know how they do. So, the shit in Kentucky ain't gonna matter. I want you to tell your lawyer to work out a plea for you."

"I told you, they don't want to talk about a plea unless I agree to testify against you."

"I know. That's what I'm getting' at. I'm going down anyway. I ain't tryna see you fall with me. I want you out on the streets to raise Tamia and Bianca."

"So what are you saying?" Her eyes glared into mine.

"Go 'head and testify against me, shawdy. It's all good."

"Nigga, how the fuck you gonna ask me to do some fuck shit like that?"

"It's for the best, boo."

"Man, you got me confused with Shan and Cheryl! I wouldn't care if those crackers offer me immunity and everlasting life. I'm still not flippin' on you."

"Listen, Inez—"

"No, *you* listen, mafucka! I was down with you when the shit was good, and I'm down with you now. Ain't no bitch ever loved you as much as me, including Juanita. Now what the fuck don't you understand about that?" She slammed the phone down on the receiver and stood up to go.

"Sit back down, shawdy," I said.

Maybe she couldn't hear me through the Plexiglas or maybe she could, but she didn't do as I asked.

When I called her collect that night she said, "I'll be back down there to see you when you got your mind right."

She hung up before I could get a word in. I grabbed a pen and paper and wrote shawdy a letter.

Dear Inez,

Shawdy, I know you ain't feelin' me on what I told you to do. Fa real, girl. I appreciate your loyalty. If only that rat nigga I fucked with was built like you, this shit wouldn't be going down. But now that it is what it is, I don't wanna see you caught up in one of these devil's cages. Feel me? See, I'm stronger than a whole nation of those devils. Put the weight on my shoulders, boo, I'll bear it. You've proven that you love me, that's enough for me. I've never told you this 'cause I really didn't realize it until circumstances separated us, but I love you, too.

Love,
Youngblood.

Four days later, I received Inez' response. A familiar scent escaped the envelope when I opened her letter.

Youngblood,

Nigga, miss me with that pity shit. Like I told you, I was down when shit was peaches and cream, and I'll be down until the end! Our daughter will never have to grow up hearing that her mother testified against her daddy.

I'm not doing it! So let's move on, please.

Baby, they're bumpin' your CD everywhere I go. I stay listening to it. I never even knew that you could rap. Boy, are you full of surprises! I love you so damn much, nigga.

Me and Juanita kicked it the other day. She's down to earth. I wanted to dislike her because, no matter what she says, she stole my man. But I like her and I know that she really loves you. I'm not mad at that. It's cool, we love the same man. Shit happens.

Boo, I'll be back to visit you again this weekend. Please don't be on any pity shit. Know that my heart is yours, always.

Love,
Inez

Shawdy was down like four flat tires.

I had the guard bring the telephone to my cell so I could call and hear her voice. After accepting my collect call, she asked, "Did you get my letter?"

"Yeah, I got it."

"Did you smell the perfume I sprayed on it?"

"Yeah, that shit smelled lovely. Did you used to spray perfume on letters you wrote to Fat Stan?" I asked, fuckin' with her.

"No. I. Did. Not," she replied, emphasizing each word. "It wasn't like that with him. I appreciated him, but I never loved him. You're the only nigga I've ever loved."

"Is that right?"

"Yep."

"You heard from Fat Stan lately?"

"Yeah, he wrote me talkin' about the situation I'm in—that's what I get for fuckin' with *you*. I wrote his fat ass back and told him to keep your name out his fuckin' mouth."

I just laughed. Fuck that hater.

"You talked to Keisha?" I asked.

"Uh-huh. Oh! She told me to tell you she would be down to see you Wednesday."

When I hung up from Inez, I called Juanita. She had gotten an apartment in Atlanta.

196

"Peace, God," she said.

"Peace. Where Justice at?"

"He's right here. Let me put the phone to his ear so you can talk to him."

Justice was eight months old now. He couldn't talk yet, but he could say *Dada*, which he kept repeating as I talked to him.

I hadn't seen any of my children since my arrest. Children under the age of sixteen weren't allowed in the county jail.

After talking to Justice, I asked Juanita to call Poochie's house for me. I was hoping Lil' T would be over there. I had received a letter from Poochie that worried me. It read:

Terrence,

As I write this letter, I pray that God is keeping you safely in His grace. I know you don't believe in my God, but He is real. And there is no other God. I know He is real because He has worked miracles for me. He delivered me from the hell of drug addiction.

I praise His name.

I pray for you every day and every night. I know that you are not the monster they portray you to be in the media. Regardless of what you did or didn't do, you are God's child.

Lil' T spent the weekend with me. He is so full of questions about what's going on with you. He sees you on the news and in the papers and kids talk about you at his school. I don't know what to tell him, he is so angry.

Shan is a mess! I wish she would give her life to the Lord. She is so messed up on drugs. I can't even trust her in my house.

About this book you say is supposed to be written. I don't mind if you tell the truth about the sins we committed together. God has already forgiven me.

He forgives all those who repent and ask His forgiveness and mercy.

With Love and Prayers,
Poochie

When Juanita called Poochie on a three-way, I was very lucky that Lil' T happened to be there.

"Lil' T! Come get the phone!" Poochie yelled.

"Who is it, Grandma?"

"Come and see."

I heard her passing my son the telephone.

"Hello?"

"What's up, boy?"

"Daddy!" he squealed.

Tears begin to swell up in the corners of my eyes.

"Daddy, is you outta jail?"

I swallowed the lump in my throat.

"Nah, lil' man."

"When they gon' let you out?"

"Probably never." I was just keepin' it real with my lil' soldier.

"Daddy, I want you to come home!" he sobbed.

That shit broke my heart.

"My friend's brother said they gonna kill you wit' lethal 'jection."

"Maybe so. But you'll always remember me, won't you?" No sense in lying to him.

Lil' T's sobs grew louder. All I could do was hurt for him. When his crying subsided he said, "If they kill you, I'ma kill them! I hate everyone who put you in jail and want you to die! When I grow up, I'ma get all them mafuckaz!"

It was like my son was no longer a ten-year-old boy, but an angry man.

"Lil' T, watch your language," I heard Poochie say in the background.

"Sorry, Grandma, but I hate everybody!" Then he burst out in tears again. "Daddy, Mama took your CD and won't let me listen to it no more. I hate her, too! My friend's brother said Mama the one who told the police on you. Did she, Daddy?"

I didn't wanna answer him because I knew the truth would turn him against his mother. I knew for certain, through discovery motions that my attorney had filed, that Shan had been the first to go to the police on me. I also knew that she was scheduled to testify against me for the state.

"Lil' T," I said soothingly, "I understand why you're so angry, but try to do this for Daddy, okay? Try not to let what people say get you so upset. You gotta be stronger than that. No matter what, know that I love you with all my heart. Be tough like I taught you. But also be smart."

"Okay, Daddy," he sniffled.

"Your mother brought you into this world," I continued. "It's your duty to love and respect her. Promise me you'll always do that."

"But she don't love *you*, Daddy," my son protested.

"That don't matter, Lil' T. Now are you gon' make me that promise or what?"

"Nope," he replied defiantly. "She told on you!"

Well, I tried. Just like me, Shan had to sleep in the bed she made. The guard told me my time on the phone was up.

"Lil', T?"

"That ain't my name no more, Daddy."

"What's your name, then?"

"Lil' Youngblood."

All of a sudden the phone went dead.

"Yo!" I beat on the cell door. "Did you cut the phone off? I asked the busta ass guard.

"Yeah. I told you your time was up."

"Bitch ass nigga, you could've let me say goodbye to my son!" I slammed the phone down on receiver, then I nearly threw it outta my cell.

When I calmed down some, I thought about my son saying that he was Lil' Youngblood. All I could do was shake my head. I did not want Lil' T to follow in my footsteps.

I felt as if I had failed him, and that burden weighed heavy on me.

CHAPTER 24

Now that I had knowledge of self, I had patched things up with Ma Duke, apologizing for allowing my pride and stubbornness to override our bond.

"Like Jigga said, I was a bastard for that," I'd told her.

"Jigga?"

"Jay-Z, Ma."

"Oh. Boy, I don't listen to that rap mess anymore."

I laughed. "Mama, you done let Raymond turn you into a square. I remember back in the day you was gettin' yo' Salt-N-Peppa on."

"Yeah, I used to bust a move or two," Mama reminisced. "Now I'm living according to the Word."

Like Poochie, Mama was on that Christian stuff, too. Although I didn't share Mama's beliefs, there was no sense in me tryna enlighten her. She was on it too hard. Anyway, I was just happy we had patched things up.

As soon as I got extradited back to Atlanta, Mama was there for me. She had been ready to sell the house her and Raymond lived in to hire Bruce Harvey, a top flight attorney, but I already had that covered.

At the county, I was allowed visits only twice a week. Mama and Juanita usually visited together.

The other day was for Inez, Poochie, Keisha, Swag and anybody else. It seemed like the whole hood wanted to visit a nigga.

Mama told me that she had drove through Englewood the other day and saw that someone had painted a mural of me on the side of one of the housing units.

"Like you're dead already!" she huffed.

"Ma, they just showing love," I explained with a chuckle.

But Mama wasn't amused. She was stressin' over the state seeking the death penalty against me.

"What gives them the right to play God?" she seethed. "And that boy's mama and sister going on television saying all that stuff like Murder Mike was a saint! *Hmmpf!* Lord forgive me, but what was you supposed to do, let them kill you?" Mama vented. She knew the laws of the streets.

"Don't let 'em get your blood pressure up, Ma. You raised a man. I can handle whatever they throw my way," I assured her." Let me recite this poem I wrote for you, Ma."

I cleared my throat, looked into my Mama's eyes through the Plexiglas and recited:

"Dear Mama,
Your work was well done
Take that from your baby, your only son
I bow my head humbly, to make amends with you.
I apologize profusely for all I put you through
I did not realize, I was unaware
I swear, Mama I wouldna took it there
When it came to loving me, you did what you felt was right
My anger and the streets blocked out your light
I couldn't see the man I was supposed to be
But through it all you kept on lovin' me
No matter what is said, when all is said and done
Hold your head high, Mama, that's from your hard-headed son."

Mama smiled and nodded her head as she wiped at the tears that ran down her face.

We said good-bye, then she left so that Keisha could visit with me alone for a few minutes. She was waiting outside in the lobby as Keisha stepped in.

Keisha said, "I shoulda been your baby mama."

"You could've been, but you swallowed all the babies," I joked.

"Ummm," she licked her lips.

"Shawdy, you need to stop." I smiled.

"Fa real though, you the livest nigga that ever lived," she proclaimed, getting teary-eyed.

"Girl, you act like you ain't coming to visit a nigga again. What's up with dat?"

"I'm good," she sniffled. "I just hate seeing you like this."

The visit ended before she could say anything more.

A week later, Swag visited, bringing sad news.

"You saw the news?" he asked.

"Nah, I ain't been watchin'."

"Sun, Keisha gone."

"Gone where?"

"They killed her."

"Slow down! What da fuck you talkin''bout? Who killed her?"

"Po-po, dawg. They swooped in on her as she pulled up in Englewood about to make a drop. Lil' Mama went out just like Latifah did in *Set It Off.*"

"Nah, man." I discounted what he said. I didn't wanna believe it.

"My word, homey." Swag put a fist to his chest. "Those mafuckaz hit ole girl with twenty-two slugs."

"Bitch ass cops!"

"I just wish she hadda took at least one with her," he said.

For the next thirty minutes we reminisced about Keisha. Swag told me that Angel was tore up over it.

I dropped my head and fought back tears as I reminisced about baby girl.

It's a'ight, lil' mama, you went out triller than a whole lotta niggaz. The streets won't ever forget that.

Swag interrupted my thoughts.

Oh yeah, homie. I forgot to tell you I found out who shot you that time at the gas station."

"Who?" I had always wondered about that.

"A nigga named PK off the Westside. Nigga braggin', talkin' 'bout he wet you up 'cause you robbed his sister and some other stripper friends of hers, said some nigga named King put him up on you."

"Oh, yeah?"

"Yep. But don't worry, the streets gon' see about dude."

"Swag," I said forcefully. "Nigga, stick to the music. What you got a chance to do is bigger than some street beef. Dude did what he was s'pose to do. I touched his people. He hollered back. Let it rest."

"I'm sayin', sun—"

"Let. It. Rest." It didn't matter now, anyway. Too much time had passed since then.

"A'ight," he reluctantly agreed.

When I got back to my cell, I wasn't even thinking about PK or what I had done to his sister. Instead, I sat down on the bunk and thought about Keisha. If only Lonnie had balls like shawdy.

I noticed three letters had been slid under my door. I picked them up and opened the first one.

Youngblood,

I will not waste time asking how you are doing. Under the circumstances, I could care less. I just need you to know that when and if you did kill Michael, you didn't just kill a nigga in the street. You killed a man. A husband. A father. A friend. Michael was all those things to me and our children. You took that all away from us. Why? Was it money? Was his friendship that cheap to you? The times you came to New Orleans with him and I welcomed you into my home, it seemed that the two of you were the closest of friends. He spoke very highly of you. Please tell me why you took him away from me?

Francisca

I set the letter down and thought about what I would say if I were to respond to her letter. I would tell her that it was Murder Mike who put shit in the game, not me. Up until he violated me, *nothing* could've made me bang him.

The code we lived by should've stopped him from going along with the Dreads' move on me. But it hadn't.

So everything that followed was fair.

I crumpled up Francisca's letter, tossed it in the commode, and flushed it.

Then I opened the second letter.

Youngblood,

You a bitch ass nigga and I hope they convict you and give your hatin' ass the needle! I'll go out dancing when they kill yo' punk ass. I always told Murder Mike that you were jealous of his shine. That's why you always tried to get him to break up with me.

Hater!

I'm still a fly bitch!

You know who.

"Cita," I said out loud.

Shawdy, you still a rat. Eat a dick!

I laid back on my bunk and opened the third letter. It was from Inez, but a fake name was on the envelope. She was just playing it safe.

Hey, boo, I miss you so much. All I do is lie in my bed and think about you, baby.

Every time I hear someone bumpin' your CD, I be like, "That's my boo!"

It seems like everywhere I go, something reminds me of you. I just wanna be able to touch and kiss you just one more time. If I could just have that one wish granted, fuck everything else.

Bitches all in my ear telling me I'm a fool for not flippin' on you. Mama tried to tell me that if you were a real man you would take all the weight and set me free. Man, we had it out! I hadn't ever cussed my mother before, but before I could stop the words from coming out my mouth, I had told her a thing or two.

She slapped the taste out of my mouth (LOL). That's okay, though. I defended you, boo. No matter what the outcome I'll never regret my decision to hold you down, nigga. Only a weak bitch turns against her man.

Mama and others keep pushing the Bible at me, telling me to pray, but after what you've been enlightening me to in regards to the science, I'm just not feeling Christianity.

Well, baby, I'ma end this letter, but never our love. It is endless...

Love, Inez and Tamia
P.S.
Trial starts soon.
Oh, boy!

CHAPTER 25

Inez was right. Our trial was scheduled to start soon.

A month after Keisha was laid to rest, autumn pushed summer out of the way, and I was taken back to Kentucky to stand trial, along with Inez, for the robbery and murder of King.

The state's case was mostly going to be riding solely on the testimony of forensic experts whose testimony would identify the bite mark on King's arm as Inez' teeth prints, the saliva swabbed from the wound as containing her DNA and hair samples found in the bed belonging to Inez.

In one of our few pretrial victories, the cruddy-faced judge ruled that my admission to Lonnie that Inez helped me setup, rob and kill King could not be used against Inez because it was hearsay, inadmissible. Lonnie would be permitted to testify to what I said I did, only.

Fearing prejudice against his client, due to all the publicity my case in ATL was receiving, Inez' attorney asked the court to severe her trial from mine, but the judge wasn't tryna hear it.

"They'll stand trial together," he ruled tersely as if he was offended by the request.

I could tell that innocent until proven guilty didn't mean shit in this old, wrinkled, cracker's courtroom. We were two blacks in *Hicktown,* Kentucky.

From the look of the jury and their expressions, once they heard the charges against us I knew we didn't stand a chance. Even the few blacks on the jury looked at us with disgust.

People like you two give all blacks a bad name! I imagined them saying.

Yeah, it was a wrap, but I guessed the DA wasn't so sure.

My lawyer proposed to me, "The district attorney says that if you'll plead guilty to malice murder and armed robbery, he'll let your codefendant plead to conspiracy. You'll get life plus sixty. She'll get fifteen, with a parole eligibility in seven."

I didn't wanna make those crackers' job easy on 'em. I knew what the outcome was gonna be, but I wanted to make them work to bam my fuckin' back out.

"I'll need to discuss this with Inez," I said.

"Let me see if I can work it out."

They let us talk in a small conference room at the courthouse. I was handcuffed and shackled. Inez, who was still out on bond, was unrestrained.

"You heard what they offering?" I asked from across the conference table that was between us.

"You look good, boo," she said, ignoring my question.

"You do, too." She was wearing a soft grey skirt suit, her hair was pulled to the back in a bun, looking like a sexy ass business executive.

"I could try to dome you off right quick," she suggested mischievously.

"You know the bailiffs and our lawyers are right outside," I reminded her. We could see them watching us through the partially closed door. "They'll be up in here so fast…"

"But at least I'll get to do a lil' somethin' somethin'."

"You would try that shit fa real, wouldn't you?" I chuckled.

"Anything for you, boo," she replied.

Okay, we'll see, I thought.

"Inez, shawdy, trial is about to start in an hour or so. This shit ain't no game. These devils 'bout to try to slam our backs out. My fate is already sealed, either here or back in ATL. Now we gotta think about *you."* Inez was looking at me like she knew what was coming next. "Shawdy, they offering a plea. Did your attorney tell you about it?"

"Yeah."

"So what's up? Can you do a bid? You'll be out in seven years."

"And *you'll* get life and sixty years. No, boo, we're in this together. Let's take it to trial. If they were confident in their case, they wouldn't offer a deal."

"I feel you, shawdy, but you don't roll the dice with these crackers 'cause if you crap out they gonna give you football numbers. I'm not tryna see you caught up like that. It was my slip with that bitch nigga, Lonnie, that caused all this shit, so let me carry the weight. Feel me?"

"No! Please don't ask me to sell you out," Inez said, eyes watering up.

"How is that selling me out? Fuck it, I'm not *asking* you to accept the plea, I'm *telling* you. If you love me, roll with me on this."

I had to put it to her like that; otherwise, she wouldn't consider it. I knew she wasn't afraid to do a bid, it was the life and sixty I'd get that she didn't wanna accept.

When I was led into the courtroom I saw all my peeps seated in the gallery: Ma Dukes, Raymond, my queen, Juanita, some of the Gods from our ciphers out West, Poochie, Lil' T, Swag and some others from around our way. Inez' mom was also there with Tamia and Bianca.

Because I wasn't handcuffed, I was able to deuce my peeps before taking a seat at the counsel's table next to my lawyer. Inez was seated at the same table two chairs away. I looked at her and tapped my chest with my fist. She blinked back tears and put a fist to her heart.

"Court's in order. Please rise!" announced the bailiff as the judge entered and took the bench.

After everyone sat back down, the judge cleared his throat and then read off a list of formalities.

"I've been informed that there will be a plea in this case?"

"Yes, Your Honor," all parties agreed in unison.

I stood before the cracker first.

After advising me that by pleading guilty I was giving up my right to appeal, blah, blah, blah, he asked how I plead to the charges of malice murder and armed robbery.

"I plead guilty."

After some more blah, blah, blah, he asked if Inez was ready to enter her plea.

"We are, Your Honor", her attorney replied.

With a cracking voice, Inez entered a plea of guilty to the charge of conspiracy to commit murder. I heard her mom cry out when the bailiff cuffed Inez.

Two days later, we were brought back to court, wearing prison jumpsuits, for sentencing.

"Do you have anything you would like to say to the court before I hand down your sentence?" the judge asked Inez.

"Yes, Your Honor. I just want to say to my daughters, who are here in court with my mother," she turned to face them. "I love y'all. Mommy will be home before you know it. To my mother, thanks for standing by me and I'm sorry if I let you down.

"To the court, all of my decisions in life have not been bad ones. I ask that you take that into consideration and that you show some mercy to my codefendant as well as to me.

"Finally, to Terrence," she said, turning so that she could face me. "I'll always love you. No one or nothing will ever make me regret loving you. Stay strong, baby," she concluded with tears.

The judge was not impressed with Inez' vowed loyalty to me. Not only did he scold her, he added an additional three years to the seven she was expecting to serve. "Because you show no remorse for the life you helped take, young lady!" he spat.

Inez' mom cried out and had to be escorted from the court-room, but shawdy took her sentence on the chin like a champ.

Me, I was heated. When I was given a chance to speak I snapped.

"You sit up there in your black robe, lookin' down on ma-fuckaz like you God. You ain't God, cracker! Who are you to pass judgment on anybody? You the devil. The black man is god! What you know about justice? With y'all it's just-us!

"Fuck *you*, the DA, the *bougie-ass* jurors who was salivating at the chance to convict us. Gimme a life sentence, cracker. So what! Y'all can't fade me. I'm the realest nigga alive!"

The cracker's face was beet red. He banged his gavel so hard it flew outta his hand and hit the reporter in her hawk-like nose. I was quickly cuffed and dragged from the courtroom.

An hour later, I was brought back before the bench. The judge's face had lightened from red to pink. He sentenced me to life plus sixty.

Whatever!

Ca$h

`

CHAPTER 26

By the time I was processed into the prison system in Kentucky and then sent back to Georgia to face the capital murder charges, winter had replaced autumn.

Back in Dekalb County Jail, I was again housed on the eighth floor in a cell alone. The solitude was all good. I had begun telling my story to a dude who planned to write a street novel based on my life, but I decided to write the book myself so that I could leave my seeds the true account of how it all went down.

Juanita was holding me down, being the true black queen that she was. She visited once a week, as she still lived in ATL. I tried to tell her to go on with her life and that it was a wrap for me but of course, she wasn't hearing it.

Ma Duke was staying strong for the most part; however, once she had broken down in tears on the phone.

"If it wasn't for my faith, I wouldn't want to live in this stinking world any longer. It was my job to protect you and Toi, and I didn't," she cried.

"Ma, you didn't fail us. I was hard-headed and didn't listen to your wisdom.

With Toi, that was my fault. My actions brought harm to her."

"Still…" she cried on.

During a visit, Swag told me that before it got cold, niggaz were wearing T-shirts with my picture on 'em with *The Realest Nigga Alive!* inscribed underneath.

Swag's CD had dropped and gone double platinum. The hottest singles were the two that I spat sixteen bars on. He broke bread with Ma Dukes and Juanita, but really they were already straight because I still had shit stashed.

Po-po would never find that. Juanita would bless my seeds with it when they became of age.

"Tell them to do the wise thing with the dough 'cause it cost me my life," I instructed. "And make sure that when I'm gone, you look out for Inez."

"I will, God," she promised.

I knew that her word was bond.

"But I'm hoping you won't be going anywhere," she said.

"It's a done deal, Queen," I said, keeping it real.

"Anyway, I already told you I prefer death over life in a cell."

"I know, baby, but—"

"No buts," I admonished through the wire-meshed Plexiglas.

Finally, the day came for the trial to begin. I wanted to discuss all the bullshit that went on to secure my conviction, but most of it didn't matter. Long story short, that rat mafucka, Lonnie, took the witness stand and sold his soul.

The bitch nigga didn't even have the courage to look at me as he testified.

The courtroom overflowed with niggaz from around our way. Niggaz that once had mad respect for Lonnie shook their heads in disbelief at the sight of him snitching. Lonnie kept his eyes glued to the floor while he relived every single murder that he witnessed me commit.

"I shoulda killed your bitch ass first!" I yelled out. "Weak ass mafucka!"

I was immediately restrained and threatened to be removed from the court if I couldn't control myself.

This the same nigga I used to think was so gangsta. But like DMX said, he's just a bitch in disguise. Just because a nigga will body somethin', that don't make him a G. Pussies kill, too.

After Lonnie hammered a nail in my coffin, the DA passed the hammer to Shan. She took the stand and sealed the deal for the state, adding a few lies to insure my conviction. The bitch didn't even care that our son sat in the courtroom listening to her rat out his pops.

"I hate you!" Lil' T screamed at her before Poochie rushed him out of the courtroom, crying.

When I was found guilty of the Lithonia killings and sentenced to death by lethal injection, Cita screamed, "Yes! I hope you die slow, mafucka!"

Out of nowhere, Ma Dukes ran up to Cita and hit her with a two-piece, sending snot flying everywhere.

Murder Mike's people were cussin' at me, applauding my fate. That set Swag the fuck off.

As the bailiff whisked me out of the courtroom, I saw that mafuckaz was tearing that bitch up.

Ca$h

CHAPTER 27

When I first arrived on Death Row at the Georgia Diagnostic Center in Jackson, Georgia, I saw my home boy, Blue, Delina's son's father who had murdered the Rib Lady and her daughter. It was instantly obvious that Blue's death sentence had blown his mind. The nigga didn't even recognize me! He was mumbling to himself like a crazy man. *Damn!* Delina sho' had poor taste in men! Blue was a busted up crackhead on the streets, a mumbling fool on Death Row. Lonnie, Delina's other nigga, was even worse. He was a fuckin' rat!

Looking at Blue, though, I knew that Death Row would never break me down like that. I was built to handle whatever.

Three Years Later...

I sat in my cell writing my last letters and completing *Trust No Man*, the book based on my life story. I had won a decision in court that stopped all further appeals of my death sentence.

For the past three years, against my wishes, attorneys had fought to have my death sentence commuted to life without parole.

"What gives them the right to appeal *my* sentence if I'm all good with it?" I had been screaming from the onset.

To the lawyers I said, "If y'all wanna save somebody's life, go down in the hood and rescue the babies. Educate my people the proper way, and stop teaching them lies!"

Still, the lawyers had fought to save *my* life.

Six months ago, at the final hour, they had gotten a stay of execution. But now it was going down. The next day at midnight I would be put to death.

Bring it on!

Out of the blue, I received a letter from Cheryl with pictures of Eryka and Chanté enclosed. The letter read:

Youngblood, I know that I'm probably the last person in the world you want to hear from, but I just had to write you. I am so sorry for what I did to you. Will you please forgive me? Because if you don't, and they carry out the execution, the guilt is going to destroy me.

Just so you know, I am no longer with the Haitian guy. Once he found out that I had all of that money, he changed, too. By then, we had twin boys and he had stolen all of the money and ran off. Now I'm back at home with Mama.

Dag!

Please don't hate me.

Cheryl

The shit was too pitiful to laugh at.

Dumb ass bitch.

I crumpled her letter and stared at the pictures of my beautiful princesses all night. I had already written final letters to each of my other children. Now I composed a letter to Eryka and Chanté.

Dear Eryka and Chanté,

My two precious princesses, you were stolen from me at a young age, so your memories of me may be few. However, my memories of both of you are plentiful and rich. If you want to know the uncensored truth about me, grab my book titled Trust No Man when it's released. Everything in it won't be favorable, especially in regards to how I treated your mother, but it will be the truth.

I've missed you both so much over the years. Now that I know where you are, and that you are okay, tomorrow night I will close my eyes in peace. I love you both.

Love,

Daddy

I prepared the letter to be mailed off and began a final letter to Inez.

Sup Inez,

Baby, by the time you receive this letter I'll be gone. I want you to know that no man has ever had a woman who's more real than you've been to me. Our time together was bliss, never an argument, never a fight. You held me down, no questions asked.

Shawdy, best believe I love you back ten-fold. I don't have to tell you to keep ya head up. You'll do that naturally because you're a rider.

Here's a surprise for you: Swag pulled some strings to get your time cut short. You'll touch down in twenty-eight months. It's official, but keep that to yourself.

You know I had to look out for my boss chick before I checked out. Remember me as I was.

Mad Love 4 U,

Youngblood

After completing the letter to Inez, I began the letter that I knew would be the toughest to write, besides the one I had previously written to Ma Dukes.

My Beautiful Black Queen,

The day has arrived when I must say goodbye to you. But remember, it is only in the physical. What we have is forever manifested in our star, Justice, and in all that we shared. How do I begin to say how very special you were to me, from the very first time our ciphers touched?

I wrote and wrote until I saw that the letter was twenty pages long. Still, there was so much more to say. Things that I wouldn't go into because best believe those devils wanted to know. Suffice it to say, though, that my seeds would be well taken care of. So with that, I put down my pen, packed my belongings, which Juanita would pick up after the execution.

Soon I would be taken to a cell across from the death room, where I would await execution under suicide watch for my last twenty-four hours.

The prison chaplain came to my cell door to request that I leave a final statement that would discourage the streets from revering me. He was concerned that I would become a martyr.

While he was bumpin' his gums I could hear Blue, who was still on death row fighting his sentence, screaming out biblical incoherencies from his cell down the range.

The Row as it was called, had snapped his mind. Some cats can handle death row, some cats can't.

"I'ma let the streets respond to my execution, however they choose to," I told the chaplain. "It is what it is."

"May God have mercy on your soul," he replied.

"I am God!" I said with a serious expression.

The chaplain frowned and then stormed away.

CHAPTER 28

Four guards and the warden led Youngblood into the state's death room at the Diagnostic Center in Jackson, Georgia. With respect for his culture, no chaplain accompanied him. Youngblood did not need a figurative crutch, he was ready to face his execution the same way he lived: *With no fear.*

He had, by stopping his appeal, told the state to bring it on. Well, tonight they were bringing it.

Juanita, Poochie and Swag were present as witnesses, per Youngblood's request. His mother declined to attend the legalized murder of her child. She wanted to be there to say goodbye to him, but she knew that they would have had to kill her, too, because as soon as they strapped her baby on that gurney she would've acted a fool.

There were three witnesses for the state also present. They sat outside the viewing window along with Youngblood's family and friends.

Juanita and Poochie held hands, giving one another strength. Swag put a hand on top of theirs. "Try to stay strong," he whispered.

Youngblood saw their faces through the viewing window. He flashed them a strong smile and tapped his heart with his fist.

As the executioner prepped him for his final seconds on earth, there was no resistance from him when he was strapped down on the gurney.

"Do you have any final words?" asked the warden, a black puppet.

Youngblood turned his head to the side so that he could see his people. The death room had a PA system so his voice could clearly be heard.

"Tell my Ma Dukes that I love her and that my choices were my own. They in no way reflect on her. Tell all my seeds that I leave here at peace because I trust that they'll be all right. Tell 'em I love them. Poochie, thanks for being here. I love you."

"I love you, too," mouthed Poochie.

"Swag, you held me down, fam. Stay thorough and you'll rape the rap game." He looked to his earth. "Juanita, baby, no words can suffice. So I'll just say you represent my legacy. You and my tribe. I love you, queen. Knowledge, knowledge," he concluded, which meant peace in their culture.

"Peace, God. I love you," Juanita said aloud.

"Hold Inez down," added Youngblood.

Juanita nodded, wiping away tears that poured down despite the strength she was trying hard to maintain.

Youngblood smiled his understanding and blew her a kiss.

"Swag," he stated, "tell the streets I said disloyalty is unforgivable and *Trust No Man.*"

Youngblood then turned his head toward the warden. "Bring it on!" he said with a brave heart.

When the death fluid was pumped into his arms, Youngblood did not flinch.

He locked eyes with Juanita and relinquished his life, dying with his eyes open, smiling at his queen.

"I love you always, baby." Juanita whispered through her tears, as she realized that Youngblood was gone.

To Be Continued…
Trust No Man 3: Like Father Like Son
Available Now!

<u>Coming Soon from Lock Down Publications/Ca$h Presents</u>

TORN BETWEEN TWO

By **Coffee**

LAY IT DOWN **III**

By **Jamaica**

BLOOD OF A BOSS **IV**

By **Askari**

BRIDE OF A HUSTLA **III**

By **Destiny Skai**

WHEN A GOOD GIRL GOES BAD **II**

By **Adrienne**

LOVE & CHASIN' PAPER

By **Qay Crockett**

I RIDE FOR MY HITTA **II**

By **Misty Holt**

THE HEART OF A GANGSTA **II**

By **Jerry Jackson**

<u>Available Now</u>

RESTRAING ORDER **I & II**

By **CA$H & Coffee**

LOVE KNOWS NO BOUNDARIES **I II & III**

By **Coffee**

LAY IT DOWN **I & II**

By **Jamaica**

PUSH IT TO THE LIMIT

By **Bre' Hayes**

BLOOD OF A BOSS **I II & III**

By **Askari**

THE STREETS BLEED MURDER **I, II & III**

By **Jerry Jackson**

CUM FOR ME

An **LDP Erotica Collaboration**

BRIDE OF A HUSTLA **I & II**

By **Destiny Skai**

WHEN A GOOD GIRL GOES BAD

By **Adrienne**

A GANGSTER'S REVENGE **I II III & IV**

A SAVAGE LOVE 1

By **Aryanna**

WHAT ABOUT US **I & II**

NEVER LOVE AGAIN

THUG ADDICTION

By **Kim Kaye**

THE KING CARTEL **I, II & III**

By **Frank Gresham**

THESE NIGGAS AIN'T LOYAL **I, II & III**

By **Nikki Tee**

GANGSTA SHYT **I II & III**

By **CATO**

THE ULTIMATE BETRAYAL

By **Phoenix**

DON'T FU#K WITH MY HEART **I & II**

By **Linnea**

BOSS'N UP **I & II**

By **Royal Nicole**

I LOVE YOU TO DEATH

By Destiny J

I RIDE FOR MY HITTA

By **Misty Holt**

Stay Connected with Us!

Text **LOCKDOWN** to 22828 to stay up-to-date
with new releases, sneak peaks, contests and more…

Made in the USA
San Bernardino, CA
20 March 2019